Praise for *Grape, Again!*

"Grape is growing up and learning some bittersweet truths in the process, but he's also the same irrepressible, hilarious, curious, one-of-a-kind kid I adored in the first book. What a joy to spend more time with him—*Grape, Again!* pops exhilarating wheelies in every inch of my heart."

- Gayle Brandeis, award-winning author of *My Life with the Lincolns*

"If you fell in love with Grape the first time around, you'll love this sequel which follows Grape's tumultuous (and sometimes hilarious) journey toward his bar mitzvah, all the while navigating the loss of his best friend and the unexpected gift of another. How will he learn enough Hebrew? Is Bully Jim a friend or foe? Will he ever learn to pop a wheelie? Young readers will delight in Grape's antics as he faces the challenges of adolescence with honesty, humor, and a big dollop of genuine wisdom."

- Meredy Benson Rice, author of *Dreamcatcher*, and *The Wisdom Palace*.

Grape, again!

Gabriel Arquilevich

Fitzroy Books

Published by Fitzroy Books
An imprint of
Regal House Publishing, LLC
Raleigh, NC 27587
All rights reserved

https://fitzroybooks.com

Printed in the United States of America

ISBN -13 (paperback): 9781646032471
ISBN -13 (epub): 9781646032488
Library of Congress Control Number: 2021943786

Interior layout by Lafayette & Greene
Cover design © by C. B. Royal

Regal House Publishing, LLC
https://regalhousepublishing.com

Printed in the United States of America

Those things
Jaymie
Those things

contents

The First Official Meeting and the Second Official Meeting

June 22, 1976

Dear Lou,

Today I tried to call you in New York.

The thing is, I really wanted to tell you about my official meeting with my mom and dad and Mrs. C. I let the phone ring a million times, but no one answered, so I went to my room and listened to Elton John, then I called again and no one answered, then I rode my new Evel Knievel bike around, then I called again, then I asked my mom why you weren't answering the phone but she didn't know.

"Maybe ask Betsy," she said.

So that's what I did.

I walked to your house and knocked.

It was super weird.

Every other time I go to your house and knock, your mom opens the door and smiles and says, "Hi, Grape. Come in. Lou's in his room," or "I'm sorry, Grape, but Lou has to do homework," or "Hi, Grape! Just in time for cookies!" but this time she kind of yelled, "Hi, Grape! What are you doing here?" because organ music was coming from the living room.

I stared at her.

The thing is, your mom had a super short haircut and she was wearing super fancy purple exercise clothes like a gymnastics lady.

"Grape?"

"Oh, I…um…I called Lou—"

"Talk louder, Grape. I can't hear you."

So that's what I did. I talked louder.

"I CALLED LOU AND LET IT RING A MILLION TIMES, THEN I WAITED AND CALLED HIM AGAIN, AND THEN I—"

"Grape, Lou is in the Catskills with his father."

"Oh. Um…"

"The Catskills are mountains."

"In New York?"

"Yes, Grape. New York isn't all tall buildings and—oh, shoot!"

The thing is, the music had stopped, and your mom looked scared. She ran inside. I didn't know what to do, so I ran inside too.

Your mom was standing in front of the TV watching a guy in a fancy PE suit and ballerina shoes. The guy said, "It's time to work on your core! Grab a chair!"

"Grape!" your mom said. "Grab a chair!"

So that's what I did. I grabbed a chair.

The PE guy said, "Now hold the top of the chair and lift your left leg up and out! On my count, here we go!" Then the organ music started, and your mom lifted her leg up and out.

"New York isn't only the Empire State Building and the Statue of Liberty and all that," your mom said. "There are mountains too."

"Like in Yosemite?"

"Yes, Grape, like Yosemite."

"Cool."

"They'll be there for a few weeks."

"Can I have his phone number? The thing is, I had my official meeting with Mrs. C."

"I know. Your mom called me first thing."

"She did?"

"Yes, Grape. She's very proud of you."

"Cool."

"But I'm sorry. Lou and his dad are staying in a wilderness

lodge. There's only one office phone for emergencies." I wanted to tell her it was an emergency. "I can give you his address," she said.

"Okay."

"I'll write it down as soon as Jack LaLanne is over."

That's the name of the PE guy.

I watched your mom hold the chair and kick her leg out. She started grunting, and then there was another exercise and she grunted more. When it was over she wrote down your address.

"He'd love it if you wrote him a letter," she said.

So that's what I did. I went home and started this letter about the first official meeting with my mom and dad and Mrs. C.

I was super nervous on the way to Mrs. C's office, but it was cool because I heard Roman the custodian's keychain jangling. He waved, then I waved, then he walked over.

"Hey, Grape! What's up? Where have you been? It's summer!"

"Well, the thing is, I went to the *1776* movie field trip, then Sherman threw up because he ate too much licorice, then Lou threw popcorn at Bully Jim, then I threw popcorn at Bully Jim, then Miss Roof kind of hopped over and grabbed my arm super hard with her nails, so I punched her—"

"Grape, is okay!" my mom said.

"Then Mrs. C suspended me for two whole weeks," I said, "and I had to write about my history of trouble and the spiders in my brain—"

"¡Grape, *no mas!*" my mom said.

"And if she liked what I wrote, I can go to regular junior high, but if she doesn't, then I have to go to Riverwash."

Roman's eyes went super wide. "The school for trouble kids?" he said.

I nodded.

"Are these your folks?" Roman said.

"Yes," my dad said. "I am Javier, and this is Angélica."

Roman shook hands with my mom and dad!

"All right then," Roman said. "Good luck, Grape!"

"Is a nice man," my mom said.

"Yeah," I said, "Roman is super cool."

We waited in the office for Mrs. C to call us in.

It was super weird.

I'd sat in that office a bunch of times before—for singing to Clair, and for changing my name, and for getting a drink of water—but I'd never sat there with my mom and dad, and the thing is, there was a new secretary and a goldfish with a super-long tail. The new secretary smiled at us.

My mom wore an Academy Awards dress and smelled like perfume and her hair was combed super straight, and my dad was wearing a suit and a tie and he didn't have his three architect pencils in his shirt pocket. They even made me dress fancy, like I was going to temple.

I watched the goldfish swim in circles, and it kind of calmed me down, and every once in a while, my mom whispered, "Is okay, Grape," and my dad coughed, not loud but not soft, either, then he patted my leg. Then I forgot about the goldfish and got nervous again because, the thing is, I didn't do much homework when I was suspended. Mostly I wrote about how I got my name, and Clair, and you, and Bully Jim, and *Butch Cassidy and the Sundance Kid*, and Miss Roof, and Sherman, and other things.

We waited a long time. I got worried that my dad might get super mad, but then Mrs. C came out of her office.

"I'm sorry for the wait. Come in, Mr. and Mrs. Borokovich."

My mom and dad stood up and shook hands with Mrs. C.

I stood up too, but she didn't shake my hand.

"I need to speak to your parents alone," she said.

I sat down and time did that slowing-down thing, so I watched the goldfish swim in circles.

"That's Barry," the new secretary said. "I've had him six years now. In fact, yesterday was his birthday."

I wanted to ask her how she knew it was Barry's birthday.

"That's pretty old for a goldfish," she said.

"Oh, um…cool."

"I got him some new marbles to celebrate. Can you see the shiny blue ones down there?" I told her I could. "You're probably admiring his tail, aren't you?" I told her I was. "He's a fancy fantail. That's the type."

"Oh, cool."

"The oldest goldfish I ever had lived almost twelve years."

"Cool."

"That's very old for a goldfish." Lou, the new secretary really likes goldfish. "I was so very sad when he died. He was floating upside down."

Then I remembered what Sherman had said about goldfish. Sometimes when they float upside down like an eyebrow it's because they ate too much, so they're just resting. "Every year," Sherman said, "thousands of goldfish are flushed alive down the sewer system or buried alive in our yards!" I thought about warning the secretary, but since she was a goldfish expert I just sat there and listened, and then Mrs. C came out and told me to bring my chair with me.

So that's what I did. I brought my chair with me.

"Take a seat, Grape," Mrs. C said.

I wanted to tell her I already took a seat, but I was too nervous, so I just stood there.

"Grape?" Mrs. C said.

"Yeah?"

"Grape, please sit."

"Oh, okay."

Mrs. C walked behind her desk. She looked at my mom and dad, then she took a deep breath and pointed at me and said, "Well, young man, I want you to know that I'm very mad at you!" But, Lou, the thing is, she was smiling. "You're the reason I didn't get any sleep last night!" she said.

I kind of slumped in my chair.

"Is okay, Grape!" my mom said.

Mrs. C pointed at a pile of papers on her desk. "Last night I started reading, and before I knew it, it was four in the morning!"

"I'm sorry."

"Is okay, Grape!" my mom said.

"And I want you to know it's worth being bleary-eyed today."

"See, Grape? Is okay!"

My dad patted my mom's leg. "Angélica, *por favor.*"

"I didn't expect a book!" Mrs. C said.

"The thing is, you told me to write one hour every day, and—"

"Your parents and I talked, and while it's true you did very little schoolwork, as long as you agree to catch up this summer, you can graduate."

Lou, my mom was wiping tears off her cheek.

My dad patted her leg more.

"Mrs. C?"

"Yes, Grape?"

"Does that mean I don't have to go to Riverwash?"

"That's exactly what it means."

So that was the first official meeting.

But that's not what I want to tell you about.

I want to tell you about the second official meeting.

This time my mom dressed a little fancy, but not like the Academy Awards. My dad also dressed a little fancy, but he had a little super-white sunscreen on his nose because, the thing is, my dad started a new hobby this summer.

Lou, my dad's super into sailing!

Every day after work he drives to Marina del Sol and takes

sailing lessons, and on Sunday he rents a boat, and all he talks about now is sailing! During dinner he teaches us how to tack, which means changing the way the sail is pointing, and he makes his mashed potatoes into a sailboat to show us what he means, then my mom says, "Javier, *por favor*," and he doesn't listen because he's super into sailing! And the thing is, he always wears a floppy hat and puts super-white sunscreen on his nose, so his nose stays kind of white, even when he goes to work and official meetings.

But my dad doesn't care.

He's super into sailing!

The new secretary was on the phone. She smiled and covered the talking part and said, "Please sit down. Principal Clarkson will be with you in a minute," so we sat in the same chairs, and I looked at the goldfish bowl.

Lou, it was super weird.

Something had happened to Barry.

His fancy tail was gone!

Mrs. C came out of her office. "Mr. and Mrs. Borokovich," she said, "so nice to see you again. Come in, please."

My mom and dad followed Mrs. C into the office.

The secretary hung up the phone and turned her chair around and opened a drawer and looked through some files.

The fish swam in circles.

"Excuse me," I said.

The secretary spun around in her chair.

"Yes?"

"Um…what happened to Barry's tail?"

Her jaw kind of dropped, then she turned back around and kept filing, then she answered like she was telling the filing cabinet what happened.

"That's not Barry," she said.

"It's not?"

"No, that's Bernie. Barry passed away shortly after his birthday."

"He did?"

She took a super-deep breath and said, "Yes, I took time off to visit my mother, and all my replacement had to do was feed him *twice* a day! A pinch of food in the morning and a pinch before leaving. That's all!" She shoved a file down super hard. "She claims to have fed him, and fed him a lot, but she must have forgotten, because the day I get back to work, poor Barry's floating upside down!"

Oh no.

"You mean like an eyebrow?" I said.

She stopped filing.

Lou, she was crying.

"Yes," she said, "that's exactly right. Like an eyebrow."

I didn't know what to do. If I told her about what Sherman said then she might think she buried Barry alive, but if I didn't tell her she might bury Bernie alive.

"Um…my friend Sherman—"

Just then Mrs. C came out of her office.

I picked up my chair and followed her in.

"Well, Grape. How are you?" Mrs. C said.

"I miss Lou. He's in New York with his dad because of what the court said."

"I'm sure he misses you too."

"But I got a new Evel Knievel bike, and I'm going to learn how to pop a wheelie, and then I'm going to learn how to jump, and I'm not going to camp this summer because Lou's not here and I have homework, so mostly I stay home and ride my bike and listen to Elton John."

"And go sailing," my dad said.

"Well," Mrs. C said, "you're probably wondering why I called you in."

"Um…yeah."

"After reading your book, I spoke with Principal Whitlock over at Lewis Junior High."

"Am I in trouble?"

"No, Grape, you're not in trouble."

"Is okay!" my mom said.

"Grape, we'd like to place you in the Advanced English class. I wanted to speak with your parents first, then get your permission."

"Um, okay."

"You would be in a double period with other kids who like to read and write." I just looked at her. "In junior high you get to choose an elective, like woodshop or music. And I know it will make you sad, I know it will be very hard for you, but you'll have to give up any idea of arts and crafts."

"Okay!" I said.

Mrs. C laughed. "No lanyards!"

Lou, Mrs. C was making a joke! She knows I hate lanyards because I told her all about it in my trouble book! Then she leaned back in her chair and laughed more, and I was laughing too because it was super funny, and my mom said, "Is okay, Grape!" and my dad just sat there. When she finished laughing, Mrs. C said, "I'm so sorry, Mr. and Mrs. Borokovich, but Grape hates lanyards!"

"Lanyards?" my mom said. "Javier, ¿qué es un lanyard?"

"Grape," Mrs. C said, "why don't you tell your parents what a lanyard is." Then she kept laughing and picked up a tissue and wiped her eyes and said, "Excuse me a moment," and left the office.

So that's what I did. I told my mom and dad about lanyards.

When Mrs. C came back, she got kind of serious. "Grape," she said, "we can't make you do this. It will be a lot of work, so it's up to you."

"It's fine. As long as I don't have to make lanyards!"

Mrs. C smiled. "Okay, then. Mr. Conway, your English teacher, will be sending a letter home, and he would like to meet you as well."

"Okay."

"But there is one more thing," she said. "Principal Whitlock strongly recommends remedial math." I just stared at her. "It's for students who need extra help, and it's also a double period." I'm bad at math so I didn't care. "Wonderful," she said. "I'm glad this is all settled."

My mom and dad stood up and shook hands with Mrs. C. But I didn't stand up.

"Grape," my dad said, "*vámonos.*"

"I…um…I need to talk to Mrs. C."

"No. The principal is very busy."

"It's perfectly fine," Mrs. C said. My mom and dad left. "Well, what is it, Grape?"

"The thing is…"

"Yes?"

"Well, it's about Barry."

"Barry? Who's Barry?"

"The secretary's old goldfish."

"Oh, I didn't know it had a name."

I explained everything to Mrs. C, and she was super nice about it.

"Don't worry, Grape, I'll make sure she knows."

"Okay. And, um…Mrs. C?"

"Yes?"

"Will Lou be in any of my classes?"

"I don't know, but I'm sure you'll see each other quite a bit."

"Cool."

"Oh, and Grape…"

"Yeah?"

"You'll work on those spiders, right?"

"Yes."

"I'm glad." I stood up. "And there's just one more thing," Mrs. C said. I stared at her. "Well, I probably shouldn't tell you this, but I *do* know someone who will be in your English class."

"You mean Sherman? He's super smart."

"Actually, no, not Sherman." Mrs. C smiled. "Grape," she said, "it's Clair."

Lou, I couldn't believe it.

It was like a miracle.

Your best friend,

Grape

The Worst Day of My Life

June 26, 1976

Dear Lou,

Today was the worst day of my life.

I did some homework for Mrs. C, then I got my Evel Knievel jacket and helmet on and started riding to the park, then a car honked at me. It was super weird.

It was my dad's car, and it was the middle of the day.

He rolled his window down and said, "Grape, come home."

"But I'm going to practice popping a wheelie!"

"You can practice later. Is important."

So I rode home.

My mom and dad were at the kitchen table. My dad had his three architect pencils in his shirt pocket, and my mom's hair was super messy, and my mom said, "Grape, is about—" then the teapot whistled, and my mom put her apron on and poured hot water in their cups and brought them over, then she took her apron off.

"Grape," she said again, "is about Lou."

She put some sugar in her tea and stirred, then she passed the sugar to my dad, then he put some sugar in his tea and stirred, then she said, "*Dios mío*," and looked at my dad.

My dad kind of just sat there.

"¡Javier, *por favor!*" my mom said, then she put her apron on again.

"Grape," my dad said, "is about Lou."

Lou, they were making it super suspenseful.

"He is staying in New York," he said.

"I know, Dad! He's in the Catskill Mountains, and they don't have a phone, so I'm writing him letters—"

"No," he said, "is more. Grape, Lou is staying with his dad."

I thought maybe my mom and dad were going crazy. My dad kept saying things I already knew, and my mom kept putting her apron on and taking it off again.

"Dad, I *know*."

"Grape, *escúchame*. Lou is not coming back. He is going to live with his dad."

It was the opposite of a miracle.

"Forever?"

"*Sí*," my mom said.

"But the court said he gets to live with his mom!"

"Is true," my mom said, "but the court change their mind."

"THEY CAN'T DO THAT!"

"Yes," my dad said, "they can. Let me put it this way…"

My dad talked for a long time and it sounded super official, but I didn't care.

"THAT'S STUPID, DAD! TELL ME WHY! WHY DID THEY CHANGE THEIR STUPID MIND?"

"Is just something that happen," my mom said.

"NO! TELL ME! I WON'T EAT AND I WON'T GO TO STUPID SCHOOL OR GO STUPID SAILING UNTIL YOU TELL ME WHY!"

My mom put more sugar in her tea and said, "*¡Dios mío! ¡Pobrecito Grape! ¡Pobrecito Lou! ¡Pobrecita Betsy!*" My dad closed the kitchen door, but the thing is, no one else lives in our house, so it was like he didn't want other parts of the house to hear, then my mom put more sugar in my dad's tea, then my dad looked at my mom and said, "Angélica, *por favor*."

"Is Betsy," my mom said. "Is nervous."

Lou, I didn't understand.

So I yelled at my mom and dad again.

Then my dad slapped his hand on the table and his teacup jumped a little.

I didn't ride my new Evel Knievel bike to the park. Instead, I went to my room and got in bed and waited to die.

Then I had a great idea.

I ran to the kitchen, and my dad had his floppy sailing hat on and his super-white sunscreen, and my mom was on the phone. She looked at me and said, "I will call you back," and hung up.

I told them my great idea.

"No, Grape," my mom said, "is impossible."

"But why? He can stay in my room. Dad, you can do a blueprint for a bunk bed and I can help you build it, and we can go to school together and when Betsy stops being nervous he can move back to his house!"

My mom and dad just looked at each other.

"I can ask the court!" I said.

"*Pobrecito* Grape," my mom said.

Like I said, Lou, it was the worst day of my life.

Your best friend,
Grape

The S-4, and Your Mom's TV is Broken

June 30, 1976

Dear Lou,

This morning I hid inside Sigmund. Sigmund is a big leafy bush in the backyard where I go to hide. Nobody knows I'm there.

Then I heard my mom say, "Grape, *¿dónde estás?*"

I didn't answer.

"Is the meeting with the English teacher!"

The thing is, I didn't want to go to the stupid meeting with the stupid English teacher.

"Okay, Grape! Is fine," she said. "You will have to do the arts and crafts."

Lou, my mom is pretty smart.

The parking lot was empty and it was super hot and all the buildings were brown and had little signs like A-1 and B-1. My mom put her sunglasses and visor on and said, "Is the S-4," so we started walking around, and my mom stopped at a drinking fountain.

Lou, I've never seen my mom use a drinking fountain before.

When she was done, she said, "Is the S-4!" again, but the thing is, we couldn't find S-4, so my mom stopped at another drinking fountain.

"*¡Dios mío!*" she said. "*¡Tanto calor! ¿Dónde está el* S-4?"

But I didn't care about the S-4.

"Hey, Mom, look!"

"Is the S-4?"

"No, Mom, look! Turkey vultures!"

"*¿Cuáles* vultures?" my mom said.

I pointed to the sky. Three turkey vultures were circling. "Everyone thinks they're eagles," I said. "Even Sherman thought they were—"

"*¡Dios mío!*" she said. "*¡No hay tiempo para los* vultures! We have to find the S-4!"

When we finally found it, my mom didn't even knock.

The teacher was sitting at his desk. He had super-curly hair like Sherman and a big mustache and a short-sleeve shirt with a pocket like my dad's, and he had super big muscles, like the PE guy on your mom's TV show.

He walked over to us.

"So nice to meet you, Mrs. Borokovich. I'm Mr. Conway." He shook hands with my mom. "And you must be Grape," he said. "I've heard a lot about you." I just glared at him. "Okay, then, why don't you have a seat?"

So that's what we did.

"Since you're joining us late, I wanted to say hello and give you your summer assignment."

I told him I don't want a stupid assignment.

"Grape!" my mom said. "*¡No le hables así!*"

"I don't blame you," Mr. Conway said. "I never wanted to read books when I was your age, but then I read *this*." He held up a book with a skinny old guy on the cover, and the thing is, the old guy was sitting on a horse, and he had armor on, and he was holding a lance, and there was a short big guy next to him sitting on a donkey, and they were both staring at an old-fashioned windmill.

"It's called *Don Quixote*," Mr. Conway said. "That's the name of the knight. The short, heavy one is Sancho Panza."

It looked super funny. Then I remembered I was mad. "Well, I don't want to read a stupid book about a stupid knight," I said.

Mr. Conway looked at my mom.

Then my mom looked at me. "Grape!" she said. "*¡Basta*

ya!" I thought she was going to talk about arts and crafts again, but she didn't. Instead, she grabbed my hand and said, "*¡Vámanos!*"

"No, it's all right, Mrs. Borokovich."

My mom sat down.

"Grape," Mr. Conway said, "why don't you take the book—"

"Is a bathroom?" my mom said.

Lou, it was super weird. I never heard my mom ask about a bathroom before.

"Yes, but I'm afraid you'll have to go to the main office. Let me draw you a map," he said.

So that's what he did.

Then my mom left.

"So, how about this, Grape? We'll make a deal. You take this book home and read one chapter."

"And what if I don't like the stupid chapter?"

"Then you'll have a choice. You can keep at it or we can move you back to a regular schedule." I didn't say anything. "Up to you," he said.

"Okay," I said. "I'll read one stupid chapter."

"And if you want to continue, answer the response questions."

"Okay."

We sat there and waited for my mom. Mr. Conway looked at his watch, then he clapped his hands together and asked me how my summer's going.

"Bad," I said. "My best friend Lou is staying in New York because the court changed their stupid mind."

"I'm sorry to hear that, Grape."

"Me, too. It's stupid." Then we just sat there more. "Mr. Conway?" I said.

"Yes, Grape?"

"I think my mom got lost again."

"I think that's possible."

When my mom finally came back she looked super hot and sweaty.

On the way home my mom was super quiet. She didn't even open her purse for a Mentos. I looked at the *Don Quixote* cover, then I read the first sentence, then the car stopped, and the thing is, we were in a parking lot.

"Hey, Mom. This isn't—"

"Is Dr. Vecchi, Grape."

Dr. Vecchi is my psychiatrist. I talk to him about the spiders in my brain. He also taught me dice baseball, the stupidest game on Earth. My mom usually sits in the waiting room, but this time she said she wanted to talk to Dr. Vecchi first. She was in there a super-long time, then it was my turn.

"Your mom told me about Lou," Dr. Vecchi said. "I'm really sorry to hear that."

"The court changed their mind."

"Yes, it did."

"It's stupid. I never saw a court change their mind in *Movie of the Week*."

"It's uncommon."

"Dr. Vecchi?"

"Yes, Grape?"

"My mom said Betsy is nervous."

"That's true."

"What does that mean?"

He leaned back in his chair and put his thumbs under his vest. "She's having a hard time, Grape."

"Does she have spiders?"

"No, it's not that."

"Will she get better?"

"Yes, I hope so."

"Then will Lou come back?"

"I don't know."

"Well, the court is stupid. Betsy is the nicest lady on Earth."

"I'm sure she is."

We just sat there, then Dr. Vecchi asked what I'm looking forward to for the rest of the summer.

"Nothing," I said.

"Fair enough, Grape. What were you looking forward to *before* you found out about Lou?"

"Riding my Evel Knievel bike and learning how to pop a wheelie and sailing with my dad and listening to the new Elton John album."

"That all sounds great," he said. "So, I guess you have a choice. You can do nothing all summer or you can learn how to pop a wheelie, and when Lou comes to visit, you can show him."

I started crying.

"I'm really sorry, Grape."

"I HATE THE STUPID COURT!"

"That's totally understandable."

"And I have to read this stupid book."

"What book?"

I told him.

"That's a great book, Grape!"

"It is?"

"Don Quixote has spiders!"

"He does?"

"He's famous for his spiders!"

"Are they trouble spiders?"

"Big time!"

"What do they make him do?"

"You'll have to read it to find out."

When we got home, my dad was in the front yard in his architect shirt and floppy sailing hat, and the thing is, he was trimming the bushes. It was super weird.

"Javier!" my mom said, "*¡Hace tanto calor! ¿Por qué estás* outside?"

My dad put the clippers down and pointed to the house. "Come with me," he said. We followed him to the front door, then we stopped. "*Escucha esto,*" my dad said.

There was organ music and a man singing and some grunting.

"*Y ahora,* look," my dad said, and he opened the door.

Lou, your mom was in the living room in her fancy purple exercise clothes with a headband and wristbands, and she was sitting in a kitchen chair pretending to row a boat, and the PE guy was on TV singing, "One, two, three, four...row, row, row your boat gently down the stream," and your mom was singing and grunting.

I thought maybe we could all hide inside of Sigmund, but we went to the kitchen instead. My dad closed the door and said, "*La televisión no sirve.*"

Lou, your mom's TV is broken.

"Now, rest!" the PE guy said.

My mom and dad sat down.

But I didn't sit down because your mom had my chair.

"Now, once more, tummy in," the PE guy said. "Do a little bicycle and I'll give you a breather!"

The organ music started. When your mom was done, she put my chair back and said the TV repairman can't come for a few days.

"Is okay, Betsy," my mom said. "You can do the Jack LaLanne here."

My dad kind of coughed.

I went to my room to read *Don Quixote.*

Your best friend,
Grape

Don Quixote Has Spiders

July 3, 1976

Dear Lou,

Dr. Vecchi is right!

Don Quixote has spiders!

The thing is, he has a giant library, but all the books are about knights, and since all he does is read, the spiders start spinning.

He makes a helmet out of cardboard and puts on old armor and rides his super-old horse into the countryside, then he gets to a hotel, but the thing is, he thinks it's a castle and the maids are rich ladies and the manager is the boss of the castle! Then he asks the manager to dub him a knight, and the manager says okay because he can tell that Don Quixote has spiders!

The dubbing has to be super official, so Don Quixote puts his armor in a horse trough and plans to stay up all night in something called a vigil, then a farmer guy takes the armor out of the trough so his mules can drink. Don Quixote gets super mad and hits him with his lance, then another farmer comes and Don Quixote almost kills him, then all the hotel workers throw rocks at Don Quixote to make him stop, then the manager guy dubs him a knight right away even though it breaks the official rules!

It's super funny!

Don Quixote's real name is Alonso Quixano, but he changes it because that's what people with spiders do! And the thing is, he's in love with a farm girl. Her real name is Aldonza Lorenzo, but he calls her *Dulcinea de Toboso*.

It's like me and Clair. *Clair de Texas.*

When I was done reading, I started on Mr. Conway's official *Don Quixote* worksheet.

1. *In fewer than 300 words, summarize the events so far.*

That was easy. I just copied what I wrote to you.

2. *Don Quixote is full of hilarious misadventures, but it also deals with serious issues. Describe one you've encountered in your reading.*

Lou, it's all super funny, so I left that question blank.

Your best friend,
Grape

My Tutor, Heidi, and Your Mom

July 8, 1976

Dear Lou,

This morning I got my Evel Knievel jacket and helmet on so I could go to the park to practice popping a wheelie, then my mom and dad called me to the kitchen table.

My dad had his floppy sailing hat on and super-white sunscreen on his nose.

"Grape," my mom said, "*quítate tu* helmet."

I took my helmet off.

My dad said, "Is a good day to be alive! May the winds be even and strong!" Then he kissed my mom on the cheek and ruffled my hair.

"Cool, Dad."

"And if the winds are not even and strong, may I have the strength to accept what comes. Let me put it this way…" He talked for a super long time, then he kissed my mom and ruffled my hair again.

I thought he was done, so I put my helmet back on.

"*Quítate tu* helmet," my mom said.

I took my helmet off again.

"*Mi hijo*," my dad said, "is news."

"Okay," I said.

"Is time to start for your bar mitzvah."

"Okay."

"But is more," my mom said.

She looked at my dad. "Javier, *por favor*," she said.

But my dad was too happy to give me bad news.

"Grape," my mom said, "is a tutor. A Hebrew tutor."

I told them I don't want a stupid tutor.

My dad wasn't so happy anymore. He took his sailing hat off, and I thought he was going to slam the table.

Then there was a knock at the door.

My dad looked at my mom. "*¡No es posible!*" he said, "*¡Angélica, por favor, haz algo!*"

"*Pobrecita* Betsy," my mom said.

Lou, it was your mom, and she was in her Jack LaLanne outfit. She was super excited about face exercises.

After your mom grunted and sang and stretched her face, my mom drove me to the temple.

The secretary said the study room is down the hall, then the second left, then the third door down.

"*Dios mío,*" my mom said, "is like the S-4!"

The thing is, it *was* kind of like S-4 because my mom stopped at a drinking fountain, and even though we were inside she kept saying, "*¡Hace tanto calor!*"

She knocked super fast and a guy opened the door and said, "Hi, I'm Aaron," and my mom said, "Is Grape," and kind of shoved me in and left.

Lou, I think my mom is nervous too.

"How's it going?" Aaron said.

"Okay," I said.

"My name is Aaron."

"My name is Grape."

"Hi, Grape."

"Hi, Aaron."

The thing is, Aaron was super calm. He didn't even ask about my name. He was also dressed all in brown, and he had calm brown hair.

"Sit down here," he said.

I sat down.

He opened a Hebrew workbook and pointed at some words.

"Can you read this to me?" he said.

I told him I couldn't.

"Can you count to ten?"

I told him I could.

"All right, go ahead."

"One, two, three—"

"No, I mean in Hebrew."

I told him I couldn't.

"But I know some of the alphabet," I said.

"Okay, let's hear them."

I said three letters.

"That's it?"

"Yes."

"You don't know much Hebrew, do you?"

"I know my name. My name is *E-nahv.*"

"That's a start. Probably won't help with your Torah portion, but you never know."

Lou, I think he was telling a joke, but I wasn't sure.

We just sat there.

"Be back in a minute," he said.

"Okay."

I looked around. I couldn't see the walls because they were filled with books. It was like Don Quixote's library.

Aaron came back with a new workbook. The cover had a bunch of little kids in a playground.

"We need to start at the beginning," he said, "like God."

I think he was making a joke again.

"Write the Hebrew letters it tells you to write, then we'll go over it."

So that's what I did.

It was super boring.

Then Aaron did something, and it wasn't super boring anymore.

He pulled a chair over to the bookshelf, then he stood on the chair, then he pulled a red book out, and the thing is, there was a magazine behind the book! He put the book back, then he sat down and put his feet up on the table and opened the magazine.

There was a fancy car on the cover, and, the thing is, three girls in bikinis were smiling and kind of petting the car.

The spiders went crazy.

Hey, Grape.

Oh no.

Hey, Grape…Do you see the cover of that magazine?

"Be quiet!" I said.

"Huh?"

"Oh, um…sorry."

Aaron kind of looked at me, then he turned the page.

"Ooh-la-la," I said.

Aaron looked at the cover of the magazine and smiled. "Ooh-la-la indeed!" he said. "I tell you what, Grape. Finish that page and I'll show you what's inside."

I worked super fast.

He looked at the page. "Oh, boy. You'll be twenty-five before you're ready."

I looked at the magazine.

"All right, then," he said. "A deal's a deal."

Lou, I was super excited.

Then I wasn't.

I thought there would be a bunch of bikini girls, but there were just super fancy *Starsky and Hutch* cars and pictures of engines, then Aaron said something about horsepower, then he took the magazine back and pointed to a car and said it was a Camaro and it was his dream car.

"I'm saving up," he said, "and when I graduate I'm going to drive across country with Sasha."

"Cool."

He opened his wallet and showed me a picture. "Isn't she the best?" he said.

"Yes," I said.

Then he asked me if I have a girlfriend.

"Um…kind of," I said.

"What's her name?"

"Clair. Clair de Texas."

He talked about Sasha more, then he showed me another car. "I tell you what," he said, "here's how you say *car* in Hebrew: *mechonit*."

"*Mechonit*," I said.

"But I guess that's kind of useless because they don't have cars in the Torah."

We just sat there.

He looked at more cars.

"How about I teach you the word for *chariot*?"

So that's what he did.

Lou, the Hebrew word for *chariot* is *merkavah*. I repeated it, then he showed me another car, then I told him about my new Evel Knievel bike and he said it was super cool.

"I'm going to learn how to pop a wheelie, and then I'm going to learn how to jump."

"That's cool."

He looked at his magazine.

"But the thing is," I said, "every time I try to go to the park, my mom and dad call me to the kitchen table."

"That's cool," he said.

Lou, I don't think he was listening.

After tutoring I got my Evel Knievel jacket and helmet on, then I opened the garage and pushed my bike to the end of the driveway and kind of waited for my mom and dad to call me back, then I pedaled super fast to the park to practice popping a wheelie.

The thing is, I have no idea how to pop a wheelie.

Evel Knievel just pulls on his handlebars and the front tire goes up.

So that's what I did. I pulled on my handlebars, but my tire only went up a tiny bit, so I tried again and the same thing happened, and it was getting super frustrating so I rode to the steep part of the gully and pedaled down super fast, then I pulled up super hard and my front tire went up.

I popped a wheelie!

The thing is, I never thought about the second part of popping a wheelie.

The tire has to land.

But my tire didn't land.

It wobbled.

I went over my handlebars, just like Evel Knievel, then my helmet hit the cement, then I rolled a few times, then I heard someone yelling, "Hey, kid! Kid!"

I kind of just rested there on the cement.

"Hey, kid! Are you okay? You crashed something brutal!"

There was a girl on a bike looking down at me.

"Ow," I said.

"Kid! Are you okay?"

"*Mechonit*," I said.

"Stay right there! I'll get your bike."

I sat up and saw her pushing my bike. She had cutoff shorts and high-tops and a *Keep-on-Truckin'* T-shirt, and the sleeves were cut off, and she had freckles all over her arms and face, and a Dodgers hat with a red ponytail sticking out of the back.

"Kid, are you okay?" she said.

"I was trying to pop a wheelie."

"Well, you're not very good at it! You pulled up way too high and you stopped pedaling and crashed something brutal!"

She got on her bike and said, "Here, watch me."

She rode up the gully, then she popped a wheelie, then she rode the wheelie down, then she landed it, then she skidded right before she got to me.

"You're super good," I said.

"Thanks. What's your name, kid?"

"Grape."

She looked at me. "Maybe you hit your head too hard."

"It's my adopted name."

"That's awesome, kid. I'm adopted too. My name is Heidi."

"Hi."

"Listen, when you're all better, I'll teach you how to pop a wheelie."

"Like Evel Knievel?"

She laughed. "Sure, like him. I can even teach you how to jump."

"Really?"

"Sure, kid, I'm here every day."

I told her I'll try, but every time I ride my bike my mom and dad call me to the kitchen table, and I have to go to stupid Hebrew tutoring and look at cars, and I have to read more *Don Quixote* and do worksheets and look for serious parts so I don't have to make lanyards.

"Wow. That's a lot, kid."

"Thank you."

"Just make sure your head's screwed on tight before you come back."

"Okay."

"And, hey, meet me at the cement slab."

"Huh?"

She pointed. "Up there, at the top of the gully. That's the upper gully, kid, where I hang out."

I pushed my bike home.

When I passed by your house I got kind of sad.

Then I looked at my Elton John watch.

It was broken.

But I still knew it was time for *Family Feud*.

Lou, I love *Family Feud*.

The thing is, your mom also loves *Family Feud*, and your mom's TV is still broken.

I got a box of Nilla Wafers and sat down on the couch next to her.

"I like your jacket, Grape."

"Thanks," I said. "It's an Evel Knievel jacket. I also have an Evel Knievel helmet."

"Did you tell Lou about it?"

I told her I did.

"Lou's father can't stand Evel. He doesn't like anything exciting."

I didn't know what to say.

Then *Family Feud* started and she got super quiet.

The thing is, my favorite part is the bad guesses, like when the British host guy says, "We surveyed one hundred people and asked them the following question: Name a place you *don't* want to ride a horse," then the person says, "in a refrigerator," and it's a dumb answer, but everyone claps and says, "Good answer!"

Lou, your mom should never be on *Family Feud*.

The British host guy said, "Name something you would take on a trip to Hawaii."

"A briefcase," the contestant guy said.

"NO!" your mom said, "CAMERA, YOU STUPID IDIOT, CAMERA!"

Then another contestant said, "A hat."

"HOW IDIOTIC CAN YOU BE?" your mom said.

A commercial came on, then she looked at me, then at the Nilla Wafers, then back at the TV, then back at the Nilla Wafers. I thought maybe she wanted one, but she didn't.

"Grape, let me tell you something. When Jack LaLanne was little he was a sugar addict. The sugar made him depressed."

"Oh, I, um—"

"It's just like alcohol."

"It is?"

"Yes, refined white sugar. That's why so many kids these days are soft and weak. Jack says they *look* like sugar."

"Oh, um, sorry."

"According to Jack, 'preservatives, salt, sugar, and artificial flavoring are the enemy of health'!"

I closed the box of Nilla Wafers.

"That's 'preservatives, salt, sugar, and artificial flavoring,'" she said again.

Family Feud started and she yelled at the TV.

Lou, she did that the whole time.

Your best friend,
Grape

The Showdown

July 11, 1976

Dear Lou,

This morning my dad was super excited to go sailing.

My mom rubbed sunscreen all over my face and arms and packed sandwiches in the ice chest, then my dad carried the ice chest to the car and said, "Is good to be alive!" then my mom said, "*Todo listo*," and my dad said, "May the wind be even and strong," then my mom said, "*Un minuto*," because she had to pee, so we waited, and my dad said, "Is good, Grape! Is good! And if the winds are not even and strong, is still good!"

Then there was a knock at the door, and it wasn't good.

Lou, your mom had her purple Jack LaLanne outfit on, and the thing is, she was holding a box and a shopping bag.

"Why, hello, Javier!" she said. "Jack promised new face exercises!"

My dad just stared.

"And I brought you a gift!" your mom said. She smiled, then my dad took off his glasses and rubbed his eyes, then he put his glasses back on and stared at your mom.

It was like a showdown from *Movie of the Week*.

"A gift for the whole family!" your mom said.

My dad stared more.

"It's a Jack LaLanne power juicer! I brought ingredients! Tell Angélica to meet me in the kitchen."

My dad and I sat on the couch. Pretty soon we heard *vroom-vroom* and your mom talking about carrots, then *vroom* again, then your mom brought us two cups.

"No more Nilla Wafers for Grape," she said, "and, Javier, no more sugar with your tea!"

The juice was terrible.

My dad didn't even try his.

We were late for sailing.

My dad drove super fast, and my mom kept saying, "¡*Despacio*, Javier!" and my dad kept yelling, "¡*Basta ya!*"

But the thing is, we didn't go sailing.

"Why the Sears?" my mom said.

"¡*No más!* Grape, *vamonos!*"

I followed my dad into Sears. He looked kind of funny with his floppy hat and super-white sunscreen, and he walked super fast through the shoe part and the clothes part and the toy part, then he got to the TV part and he said, "¡*No más!*" kind of loud, and people looked at him, then he bought a TV and the worker guy helped us put the TV in the car.

But we still didn't go sailing. Instead, we drove home.

My dad got the dolly from the garage. He put it in the car, then we drove to your house, then my dad said, "Grape, hold the dolly," so that's what I did, then my dad put the TV on the dolly and pushed it to your front door and knocked.

No one answered.

There was *vrooming* inside.

My dad knocked super hard.

The *vrooming* stopped.

"Just a minute!" your mom said.

My dad knocked again.

"Who is it?" your mom said.

"Is Javier."

"And Angélica," my mom said.

"Is everything all right?"

"Is okay!" my mom said.

"I hope you like your juicer!"

My dad knocked again. This time your mom opened

the door, but just a little. Lou, it was super weird. She was wearing a robe and she had mud all over her face. She looked down at the box. "What is it?" she said.

"Is a present!" my mom said.

"A TV," my dad said.

Your mom's eyes got super wide, and it was kind of scary because of the mud all over her face.

She walked back inside the house.

We followed her in, and then your mom sat down, and the thing is, her TV was on.

Lou, her TV was working.

I thought my dad would say *¡Hijo de puta!* but he didn't.

Then my mom did something. She kneeled in front of your mom and hugged her, and your mom sob-cried, and when she was done, there was mud on my mom's face too.

My dad and I just stood there, and then my dad did something super cool.

He invited your mom to come sailing with us.

It was the best trip ever. The wind was even and strong, and I only threw up once, and your mom wore a life jacket the whole time.

Your best friend,
Grape

Tʜᴇ Uᴘᴘᴇʀ Gᴜʟʟʏ, ᴀɴᴅ ᴛʜᴇ Mɪʀᴀᴄʟᴇ ᴀʙᴏᴜᴛ Mʏ Mᴏᴍ

Jᴜʟʏ 22, 1976

Dear Lou,

Today I rode to the upper gully. It's past the T-ball field and the Little League field where there's nothing but weeds and chaparral, and at the very top there's a cement slab.

That's where Heidi hangs out.

"Kid! Hey, kid! Up here!"

She wore a shirt with a big fancy YES on it, and she was sitting next to a guy with a black beanie on even though it was super hot, and he was sitting next to a boom box.

"Kid! You came back!"

I just looked at her.

"Kid? Are you okay?"

The thing is, she was holding a cigarette.

The smoke was drifting across her face.

She took a puff and passed the cigarette to the guy with the beanie, then he took a puff, and then she ran to me and said, "Kid!" a bunch of times.

"Hey, Rusty," she said, "this is the kid I was telling you about!"

"What's up, man?" Rusty said, and smoke came out of his mouth.

"Um…I crashed."

"You crashed something brutal!" Heidi said.

"Cool, man," Rusty said.

"Hey, kid, tell me your name again."

"Oh, um…Grape."

"Cool name, man," Rusty said.

"Thanks."

"How's your head, kid?" Heidi said.

"Okay, but my Elton John watch broke."

Rusty took another puff of the cigarette and blew a smoke ring.

It was super cool.

Then he said something not super cool.

"Elton John sucks."

I was scared and mad at the same time.

"You ever heard of Black Sabbath?"

I told him I hadn't.

"They rock," he said.

"I know KISS," I said.

"KISS sucks too," he said. "Poser AM music."

Lou, I'm glad you weren't there.

"Listen to this," he said, then he pressed a button on the boom box, and this guy started scream-singing, then someone played guitar for a super long time.

"That's real music, man. None of this AM poser crap."

"Leave him alone, Rusty."

Rusty turned off the music.

Heidi, Queen of the Upper Gully.

"So you want to practice that wheelie now?" Heidi said.

"Okay."

"All right. Follow me."

We rode to the little league field.

"You're gonna crash, kid, so grass is better, and before we start, we have to adjust your seat. You want low gravity."

Lou, Heidi's a bike expert.

She was right. I crashed a bunch of times, but I kept trying, and then Heidi asked me what time it was.

"I don't know. My Elton John watch broke."

"Oh yeah."

She looked up at the sky kind of serious. "I better go," she said. "My new parents are brutal strict." Then she took a cigarette from behind her ear and put it in her mouth and lit it. "Come back tomorrow, kid?"

"I'll try. The thing is, I have to read *Don Quixote* and try to find a serious part, then I have Hebrew tutoring, then I have homework for Mrs. C."

"I have homework too, kid."

"You do?"

"Yup. Makeup credits."

"Um…what school—"

"Riverwash," she said.

Lou, I couldn't believe it.

"And after you get the wheelie down," she said, "I'll teach you how to jump."

"Really?"

"Sure!"

"Okay."

"I better go. My new parents are brutal strict." Lou, that was the second time she said that.

Then she said something else.

"Come back tomorrow. Love you, kid."

But I couldn't come back tomorrow. Instead, I had to go sailing.

My dad woke me up super early. He was wearing his floppy hat and had super-white sunscreen on his nose. *"¡Mi hijo!"* he said. "Is a good day to be alive! Today we are renting the thirty-five-footer! Eat breakfast and we go! Is different! It has companionway and a kitchen table and radio! Is like a house inside! Grape, it has companionway!"

Lou, my dad's super into the companionway.

The thing is, I wanted to ride bikes with Heidi.

"I don't want to go," I said.

He just looked at me.

The companionway is the opening that goes into the boat.

It has a little ladder you climb down. And the thing is, my dad was right. It *was* like a house inside. It had a fridge and a stove and a sink and a kitchen table and padded seats, and the kitchen table folds down so the seats turn into a bed.

"Well, Grape, what do you think?"

"Cool," I said.

"Up the companionway!" he said.

He started the engine and we motored out of the harbor, then he pointed to the tailpipe thing at the end of the boat.

"Grape," he said, "is water spitting out?"

I looked at the tailpipe thing.

"Yes," I said.

"*Muy bien*," he said, "the engine is cooling."

I put my head on my mom's lap until my dad said, "Angélica, *maneja por favor*," then my mom put a cushion under my head and steered, and my dad walked on the deck and pulled on a rope so the sail went up, then he turned off the engine and steered, then I put my head on my mom's lap again and got super sleepy, then my dad said, "Angélica, *maneja otra vez*," so my mom put the cushion back and steered, then my dad started singing super loud, and I heard another sail going up, then more singing, then we sailed for a while, then my mom started yelling, "*¡Dios mío,* Javier, *basta!*"

It was super weird. I'd never heard my mom complain about my dad's singing before.

Then my mom yelled more.

I opened my eyes.

Lou, my dad was on the deck. He was wearing tennis shoes and his floppy sailor hat.

But that was all.

Lou, my dad was streaking!

I closed my eyes.

Then I opened them.

He was still streaking!

My mom yelled, "Grape! Take the tiller! Take the tiller."

So that's what I did.

I thought she was going to yell at my dad more, but she didn't. Instead, she threw up over the side of the boat.

When she was done there was a little throw-up on her chin and she was super pale, then she said, "*Por favor*, Javier," kind of soft, and my dad stopped singing and got dressed.

Then my mom threw up again.

When we got home I put my Evel Knievel jacket and helmet on.

I didn't even make it to the garage.

My mom was at the kitchen table in her pink robe and slippers and her hair was super messy, and the thing is, she didn't have her apron on, and my dad was holding her hand.

"*¿Necesitas algo?*" my dad said.

"No, Javier, *estoy bien.*"

"*¿Un poco de te?*"

"Okay."

Lou, my dad made tea for my mom.

It was super weird.

Then he closed the kitchen door.

"Grape," he said, "is news."

He was super serious.

Then he looked at my mom. "Angélica, *por favor.*"

My mom started to cry a little, then she said, "*Mi hijo*, is news, I am—"

Then she ran out of the kitchen.

"Dad?"

"Is okay, Grape."

We sat at the kitchen table and listened to my mom throwing up.

When she came back she just looked at me and stroked my cheek and said, "Grape, is okay."

I didn't understand.

Then I did.

"Is a baby," my mom said.

Lou, my mom is pregnant.

My jaw kind of dropped.

My mom hugged me and her tears went down my cheek and she kissed me and said, "*¡Es un milagro!*"

"Grape," my dad said, "when the winds of life change, you steer with the changes. Let me put it this way…" He talked for a super long time, and my mom cried and stroked my cheek, then she ran out of the kitchen, then we heard her throwing up more, then it was quiet, then it wasn't quiet.

"Many things are happening," my dad said. "Grape, is good to be alive!"

I went to my room to read *Don Quixote*.

Your best friend,

Grape

Camp Grape, Radishes, and Heidi

August 17, 1976

Dear Lou,

My life is like camp now.

Camp Grape.

I do everything the same.

I wake up and read *Don Quixote*, then I do the worksheet and try to find a serious part, but I can't, so I leave that part blank, then I eat lunch, then my mom drops me off at temple and says, "*¡Dios mío, tanto calor!*" then I sit in the study room and Aaron says, "We really have to get something done today," like it's a super-calm emergency, then the spiders say, *Hey, Grape, bikinis!* and I say, "Ooh-la-la," and Aaron shows me a bikini picture from his car magazine and talks about Sasha and the new Camaro, then he says, "Man, time flies," and teaches me a Hebrew word, then my mom waits for me in the parking lot with the air conditioning on, then she gives me a Mentos and drives me home, then I get my Evel Knievel outfit on and ride to the cement slab to practice popping wheelies with Heidi, then I ride home, and if your mom's not there I watch *Family Feud* and eat Nilla Wafers, then my dad comes home, then we have dinner and talk about names for the baby.

But today Camp Grape was different.

Today, *Don Quixote* had a serious part.

After being dubbed a knight, he rides home to find a squire because that's what knights do, but on the way he sees this boy named Andrew tied to a tree, and the thing is, his shirt's off and he's being whipped by his boss! Don Quixote tells the boss to set him free or else, but the boss says that

Andrew keeps losing his sheep and that's why he has to whip him, but Don Quixote doesn't believe him, so the boss unties Andrew and Don Quixote makes him promise to be nice from now on, so that's what he does, and then Don Quixote rides away and he's super proud of saving the boy.

But the thing is, he didn't save the boy.

That's the serious part.

After Don Quixote rides away, the boss ties Andrew to the tree again and whips him extra hard and makes fun of Don Quixote the whole time.

In my official worksheet I wrote about how spiders can make you do dangerous things like climb into a storm drain because of an orange golf ball or streak a little or throw popcorn at Bully Jim.

Then I went to Hebrew tutoring.

Hebrew tutoring was also different.

Aaron kept looking down and sighing and saying, "Ugh," and when I said, "Ooh-la-la," he said, "Not today, Grape. Today, just do your workbook."

I opened the workbook and copied a few words.

Aaron ran his hand through his hair, then he put his hands on his face and said, "Ugh."

It was super dramatic.

But the spiders didn't care.

"Ooh-la-la," I said.

"All right, *ooh-la-la, ooh-la-la*, who gives a whatever."

Aaron got the magazine and threw it down in front of me, then he sighed and put his hands on his face again and said "Ugh" a bunch of times.

I didn't know what to do, so I told him my mom was going to have a baby.

"Ugh," he said.

Then he said another word.

"Sasha."

I just sat there.

"She said I'm too chilled out."

He talked for a long time, but his hands were on his face so the words came out kind of blubbery.

I opened the magazine and looked for bikini girls, then he told me never to have a girlfriend. I asked him about a car because I thought it would cheer him up, but he just put his head down on the table and said, "Ugh. Sasha."

He didn't even teach me a Hebrew word.

Like I said, Camp Grape was different.

Then it got even more different.

My mom wasn't in the parking lot with the air conditioner on. Instead, she was in the waiting room, and my dad was with her, and my mom was dressed kind of fancy, and my dad was in his work shirt with his three architect pencils.

"Today we meet with the rabbi," he said.

"We do?"

"Yes! Is important day, Grape."

The thing is, I wanted to see Heidi.

"How come you didn't tell me?" I said.

My dad just looked at me.

The rabbi came in, but the thing is, he didn't look like a rabbi. He didn't have a beard, and he had fancy circle glasses, and he wasn't wearing a yarmulke. He shook hands with my mom and dad.

"So nice to meet you, Mr. and Mrs. Borokovich."

"Is a pleasure, Rabbi, so much," my dad said.

"I hear your family has good news!"

"Yes, Rabbi," my mom said. "Is a miracle!"

"And you must be *Gav-ree-el*," the rabbi said.

"My name is Grape," I said. "*E-nahv.*"

My dad took a deep breath.

"It's my adopted name," I said.

"Well, okay, then, Grape. It's a pleasure to meet you. I'm Rabbi Len."

I shook his hand.

It was super weird. I never shook hands with a rabbi before.

"I hear you've been working hard with Aaron," he said.

Oh no.

"He studies every day, Rabbi," my dad said.

"Wonderful. We start on your Torah portion soon. It's a good one. Moses parts the Red Sea."

"Is a miracle!" my mom said.

"Do you know that story, Grape?"

I just looked at him.

I knew that story, but I hated it. The thing is, Moses reminds me of Passover, and Passover reminds me of radishes.

Lou, I hate radishes.

But my dad loves Passover.

It's super official. There's an official plate of food with matzah and a bone and an egg and parsley and salt water and a kind of apple thing and a radish, and since I'm the youngest, I have to read a bunch of official questions about why Passover is super important, then we eat.

I like matzah and egg and parsley and the apple thing, but every year I skip the radish.

Except last year.

Last year my dad looked at my plate and said, "Grape, you will eat the radish."

I just looked at him.

"Javier," my mom said, "*no importa.*"

My dad slammed his hand on the table. "*¡Come el* radish!*" he said.

I took a little bite, and I thought I would throw up, so I spit it out.

"*¡Cómelo!*"

I didn't know what I'd done wrong. I mean, I'd never had to eat the radish before. I stared at my plate and my dad pointed again and told me to eat, then my mom said, "*¡Javier, basta!*" and she took the plate with the chewed-up radish to the kitchen.

So, Lou, that's why I don't like radishes.

"Grape!" my dad said, "the rabbi is asking a question!"

I told the rabbi I knew the story.

"We'll focus on what happens *before* the parting of the Red Sea, because what happens before an event is important."

"Yes, Rabbi," my dad said, "what happens *before* is very important. Let me put it this way—"

"Javier!" my mom said, "*por favor.* Is not your bar mitzvah! Is Grape's bar mitzvah."

The rabbi kind of laughed.

When I got home I put my Evel Knievel jacket and helmet on and rode to the park and popped a wheelie on the way.

Three times!

Lou, I'm super good at popping wheelies!

Then I pedaled up the steep part of the upper gully.

"Hey, kid!"

"Hi, Heidi! Check out my wheelie!"

The thing is, I could do a regular wheelie, but I never tried an uphill wheelie before.

I crashed something brutal.

Heidi asked me if I was okay.

I said I was, then she walked me to the concrete slab.

"Was that your first uphill wheelie, kid?"

I told her it was.

"Don't pull so hard next time, and pedal faster."

"Okay."

"Here, watch me."

She rode down the gully and then she rode back up and popped an uphill wheelie.

"Want to try?" Heidi said.

"Um…"

"That's all right, kid. Take a break."

So that's what we did. We took a break.

Rusty played Black Sabbath and told me to listen to the lyrics.

Heidi said I crashed something brutal.

They smoked a cigarette.

It was super boring.

"Can we practice jumping?" I said.

"You sure you're okay?"

"Yes."

We rode to the Little League grass and Rusty set up the ramps, then Heidi told me to make myself light and keep my tires straight and land soft, then she jumped two cans, then Rusty jumped two cans, then she said, "Your turn, kid. Remember, make yourself light."

I tried to make myself light, but it didn't work.

"You really are like Evel Knievel," Rusty said.

"Almost," Heidi said. "Keep pedaling after you land. Make yourself light, kid."

I crashed three more times, then I made it!

"Great, kid! You made yourself light!"

I jumped a bunch more and landed it every time, then Heidi said we should take a break.

So that's what we did.

It was super boring.

Then I remembered something.

"My mom's going to have a baby," I said.

"Really?" Heidi said.

"It's a miracle."

"I'm happy for you, kid."

"Thanks."

Then Heidi said she had to go. "My new parents will kill me if I'm late," she said.

That's the third time she said that, so I asked her.

Lou, the thing is, Heidi's a foster child.

"I've had five moms and dads," she said. "Can you believe

that? I even lived in Texas with my older sister for a while."

I asked her if she knew Clair.

"Who?"

"Clair. The thing is, she's in my class and she's from Texas, and there's a super famous song called "Clair," and Miss Roof kicked me off the whale-watching trip because I was singing the Clair song instead of doing math."

"Texas is pretty big, kid," she said.

She lit a cigarette.

"Anyway," she said, "I'm aging out, and I don't know what's next. It's up to my new parents and the court."

"I hate the court," I said, then I asked about her real mom and dad.

She took a puff of her cigarette and held it in a long time.

"Enough questions," Rusty said.

"It's all right," Heidi said. "My dad was a no-show, and my mom couldn't handle a kid."

"Was she nervous?"

"You could say that."

"Um…where is she now?"

Heidi took another puff then scraped the cigarette on the cement and it made a black line. "She's dead, kid. So, lucky me. I've had lots of moms and dads."

Then she got kind of quiet.

I just sat there.

"Hey," she said, "you want to ride to the playground? I'm brutal thirsty."

"Okay."

At the playground Heidi drank a super long time, then I drank a super long time, then we sat on our bikes, then Heidi pointed at the sandbox.

"Kid, you see that turtle?"

Lou, she meant the big clay sandbox turtle.

"A pro could take off from the edge of the sandbox and jump it. No ramp or anything."

"Cool!"

"That's what I mean by making yourself light," she said.

"Cool!"

"Landing in the sand might be a problem, but you get my point, right, kid?"

"Yes!"

We sat on our bikes.

"I better go," Heidi said, "or my new parents will kill me."

I didn't know what to say.

"See you tomorrow. Love you, kid."

I looked at the turtle again, then I rode home.

Your best friend,

Grape

Orientation

Dear Lou,

Today I had junior high orientation.

I sat next to my mom on the gym bleachers. I was kind of nervous, then I saw Sherman sitting next to his dad, then I waved, then he waved, then I felt better, then I looked around for Clair but I couldn't see her. Then I was worried that she'd moved back to Texas. And the thing is, it was super hot, and one of the lights was buzzing, then a lady with a microphone said, "Welcome students!"

She waited for people to clap, but no one did.

"Let me introduce Principal Whitlock!" she said.

A man with a fancy suit and a big belly kind of skipped across the gym floor. He was bald except for the back of his head. The lady gave him the microphone and looked up at the buzzing light and frowned.

"Thank you, Amanda! Parents and students, welcome *again* to George A. Lewis Junior High School!"

He sounded like a game show host.

He talked about transitions in life, then he wiped his forehead with a handkerchief and talked more, and it was super boring. "And without further ado," he said, "here's Amanda to tell you about the rest of the festivities!"

He handed the microphone back to Amanda and wiped his forehead again.

"On your way out," Amanda said, "stop at the tables to get your book locker assignment and combination as well as your PE uniforms, then proceed to your first period class, which will begin at 9:30 sharp. When the bell rings, you'll have four minutes—that's *four minutes*—to get to your second period class. This mimics your daily schedule."

Lou, junior high is super official.

My first class was Advanced English.

"Is the S-4," my mom said. "*¡Vamanos!*"

Mr. Conway said hello and shook hands with my mom. It was just like our first official meeting, except this time Mr. Conway wore a tie and the walls were decorated with posters of people's faces with words under them.

"Nice to see you again, Grape," Mr. Conway said. "How have you been?"

"My mom's having a baby," I said.

"Grape!" my mom said, "*¡qué cosa!*"

Mr. Conway laughed. "That's wonderful news. Congratulations. And I take it you're enjoying *Don Quixote*?"

"Yes," I said. "It's super funny."

"I agree!"

"And his spiders are a lot worse than mine."

"Spiders?"

I started to tell him about the spiders in my brain, but then the classroom started to fill up. Some of the parents sat in the kids' chairs and some stood in the back. When it was 9:30 sharp, Mr. Conway said it was an honor to be able to spend a school year with us.

"I'm not going to bore you with our curriculum," he said. "It's too hot for that."

Some of the parents laughed.

"But if you do have any questions," he said, "now's a good time."

A lady with a super fancy hat and freckles on her shoulders raised her hand and asked why her daughter's being asked to read *Don Quixote*. And the thing is, she had a Texas accent, and a girl with a super fancy hat was sitting next to her.

It was Clair's mom!

And if it was Clair's mom, it was Clair!

She had a pretty green dress on, and her face was super red.

"I don't understand your question," Mr. Conway said.

"Well, it's amusing and all, but these are twelve-year-old children. The innkeeper scene, for example. My daughter and I more or less skipped it."

Lou, Clair's mom was talking about the vigil when Don Quixote beats up the mule guy!

"I'm sorry to hear that," Mr. Conway said. "It's a wonderful episode."

I agree!

"But is it appropriate?"

"If you mean, is it appropriate for Advanced English students to read stories with prostitution, I say sure, in the right context, it is. Otherwise I wouldn't assign it."

Lou, I had no idea what he was talking about.

"Yes, but—"

"Also, students read on their own. No parents. The instructions are in the mailing I sent."

The bell rang.

Four minutes!

"You can ignore that," Mr. Conway said. "This is a double period. Feel free to look around the room."

So that's what I did.

I looked around the room. For Clair.

She was staring at a poster of a lady with a super sad face, and under her face it said,

> This is my letter to the World
> That never wrote to Me—
> The simple News that Nature told—
> With tender Majesty

I said hi.

Clair said hi.

I tried to say something else, but my tongue was kind of sticking to the roof of my mouth.

Then Clair said, "Grape, this is my mom."

Lou, I shook hands with Clair's mom!

Then I said, "Clair, this is my mom."

"Is the song!" my mom said.

Clair turned super red again.

We all just kind of stood there.

"Why don't you tell your friend about your summer?" Clair's mom said.

"I was in Texas," Clair said.

"And?"

"And I played my violin."

"And?"

"And I won a competition. There, I told him."

"My Clair won first prize in county," Clair's mom said.

"Is very good, Clair," my mom said.

"Thank you," Clair said.

Then Clair's mom asked how I spent my summer.

So I told her.

Clair and her mom just looked at me.

"Oh, and my mom's going to have a baby," I said.

Then the bell rang.

Four minutes!

Lou, my science teacher is super weird.

His name is Mr. Frasier, and he's tall and his head is square, and he has a crew cut like an army guy. He stood behind his desk saying, "Choose any station" over and over because there weren't any desks, just tables with stools, and the thing is, there was a skeleton hanging in front of the chalkboard.

Then something cool happened.

"Hi, Grape!"

It was Sherman!

And then something uncool happened.

"Hey, Grapeface."

Bully Jim was sitting at my station, and the thing is, his

hair was short and combed, and he wasn't even wearing a tough-guy flannel.

When the room was full, Mr. Frasier kind of stood there and waited, and it got super quiet, then he walked behind the skeleton!

"Good morning," he said, "I'm Mr. Bones. Mr. Frasier couldn't make it today."

And the thing is, he moved the skeleton arms when he talked!

Everyone laughed.

"*¡Qué cosa!*" my mom said.

Mr. Bones talked about our science units, but the longer he talked, the more boring it got, and people stopped laughing, except for Sherman.

Sherman cracked up the whole time, and his dad was laughing too.

Then the bell rang.

Four minutes till PE!

We met in the boys' locker room.

The PE teacher wore sunglasses even though he was inside, and sweatpants and a tank top, and when he talked the veins in his neck bulged out and his voice kind of echoed off the walls. "I'm Coach Ruth," he said. "Head of athletics. Head of intramurals. Proud alumnus of George A. Lewis."

He paused, but nobody clapped.

"Fell in love with cross country right here. Started with six-minute run. On to Castillo High. Two state championships. Scholarship, Cal State Long Beach. Teaching credential, on to—"

"*Dios mío,*" my mom said, "*tanto calor.*"

Coach Ruth kind of looked at her.

"On to student teaching. Landed a spot here. Dream job. Any questions?" Nobody had any questions. "All right, then," Coach Ruth said. "Three rules. Real simple. Rule number

one, buy a lock. Lock is for your locker. Memorize combo.
Lock up belongings. Any questions?"

Nobody had any questions.

"Rule number two, always dress out. Even if not
participating. Don't dress out, *do* get an absence. Absences
affect grades. Questions?"

Nobody had any questions.

"Rule number three, see those showers behind me?
Mandatory. No exceptions. Two minutes in and out. That's
three simple rules. Lock, dress out, shower."

"*¡Tanto calor!*" my mom said.

She looked super pale, like she might faint.

Then I saw someone else who might faint.

It was Sherman.

The thing is, Sherman has a super thick scar from his
chest all the way to his belly. I saw it when we tried out for
the Hawks. We had a shirts-versus-skins scrimmage, and we
were on Donny Randall's team, which was super cool. But
we were also skins, which was super uncool. Sherman had to
take his shirt off and everyone saw his scar.

Coach Ruth talked more about PE and combinations, but
I can't remember what he said.

I was looking at Sherman.

The only thing left was math, but we never made it.

"*No más*, Grape," my mom said.

Lou, sometimes it's cool that my mom is pregnant.

Your best friend,
Grape

My First Day of School

August 25, 1976

Dear Lou,

Mr. Conway is cool.

The first day of class most teachers take roll and talk about the rules and give us books and tell us to cover them, but not Mr. Conway.

"I'm going to point at you," he said, "and you'll number off one through six. The ones meet by the Hemingway poster, twos by the Shakespeare poster, threes by the Dickinson…."

It was like math, but I understood.

I was a three.

And so was Clair!

"Introduce yourself, then share what you did this summer and your favorite scene in *Don Quixote* so far. When I ring this bell, it's the next person's turn."

Clair went first, but I forgot what she said because I was looking at the freckles on her shoulders.

Then it was Maxwell's turn.

Maxwell has super-blond hair that looks like a big wave with a bunch of little waves in it. He went to Crestline Academy and spent his summer in England, and he got to watch a rugby match, and his favorite part of *Don Quixote* is when he attacks the windmills.

Then it was my turn.

"I'm Grape," I said.

"That's your name?" Maxwell said.

"It's his adopted name," Clair said.

"Weird," Maxwell said.

"This summer I had two official meetings with Mrs. C and

one with Mr. Conway and one with the rabbi, and I learned how to pop a wheelie even though I crashed a bunch of times, and I'm practicing for my bar mitzvah and getting extra tutoring because I'm bad at Hebrew, and my best friend Lou is staying in New York because of the stupid court, and my dad's super into sailing, and my mom's going to have a baby."

Everyone stared.

"My favorite part of *Don Quixote*," I said, "is when he makes people say Dulcinea de Toboso is the most beautiful lady in the world."

I looked at Clair.

But the thing is, she wasn't looking at me.

She was looking at Maxwell.

The rest of class we discussed our worksheets, then Mr. Conway passed out a poem called "I'm Nobody! Who are you?" by Emily Dickinson, the sad-faced lady on the poster. The poem is about being nobody instead of a frog, and the thing is, she uses dashes instead of periods or commas, and she capitalizes any word she feels like capitalizing.

Lou, I didn't understand it at all.

But there was someone who did.

"I *love* that poem!" Clair said. "Sometimes I just want to be alone and not worry about school or violin or *anything!*"

Then we read another Emily Dickinson poem. It starts like this.

> "Hope" is the thing with feathers—
> That perches in the soul—
> And sings the tune without the words
> And never stops—at all—

Clair raised her hand.

Then the bell rang.

"Remember," Mr. Conway said, "the classroom is open during lunch. If you need help or just want to hang out, I'm here."

I ran to science.

Mr. Frasier took a long time to take roll. The thing is, he's super interested in last names.

"Allen?"

"Here," Bully Jim said.

"If I'm not mistaken, Allen's a Scottish name?"

Bully Jim didn't care.

"Borokovich?"

"Here, sir!" I said.

"Borokovich, that's no doubt Russian?"

"Um…my mom and dad are from Argentina."

"Yes, it must be." He scratched his chin and said, "Yes, it must be" again, then he walked behind the skeleton and kept taking roll.

A few kids later he said, "Kaufman?"

"Here, Mr. Bones!" Sherman said. "Right here!"

"Kaufman…Kaufman…that must be—"

"It has a German origin. My ancestors come from a line of Ashkenazi Jews," Sherman said, then he talked a long time and Mr. Bones kept saying, "I see." When he was done with roll half the class was over.

Then he said it's time for our textbooks, but instead of asking for help handing them out like a normal teacher, he passed them out one by one and dropped them on the stations so they made a thump.

"Book covers by Friday," he said.

Thump. Thump. Thump.

"Of course, Admin won't invest in new books, but they can give themselves raises!"

Thump.

"And who bought chalk for his own class? Frasier did. That's who!"

He got behind the skeleton again.

"Are there any questions for Mr. Bones?" Mr. Bones said.

Lou, you wouldn't believe it! Bully Jim raised his hand.

"When do we cut up the frogs?" he said.

Mr. Bones waved his skeleton arms. "Have some respect for the dead, young man!"

Sherman gasped and pointed.

"Oh, sorry," Bully Jim said.

"The correct term, Mr. Allen, is *dissection*. Would you like to ask your question again?"

"Yes, ask it again!" Sherman said.

Bully Jim kind of looked at Sherman.

"Okay," Bully Jim said. "When do we dissection the frogs?"

Mr. Bones told him.

"Cool," Bully Jim said.

"Of course, only if it's in Admin's budget. You never know with Admin. Frasier might have to catch the frogs himself!"

The bell rang.

Four minutes!

I ran to my book locker and spun the combination wheel super fast, then I felt a tap on my shoulder.

"Cool about the frogs, huh, Grapeface?"

"Um...yeah."

"We get to cut them up."

"Yeah."

"But bummer about no dodgeball courts."

"I know. Bummer."

"What classes do you have?"

I told him.

"Cool."

Then he told me about his classes, but I didn't care.

"Um...the thing is, we only have four minutes! It's official!"

I opened my locker and got my PE clothes out.

"Hey, but, Grapeface?"

"What?"

"Where's Lou-Lou?"

I told him.

"Bummer. Okay, see you at lunch."

I closed my book locker and spun the combination wheel, then there was another tap on my shoulder.

It was Sherman.

"It's time for PE!" I said. "We only have four minutes!"

"Well, you better hurry up then, Grape!"

Sherman just smiled.

"No PE for The Sherm!" he said.

"What do you mean?"

He pulled a tiny black suitcase out of his backpack.

"Do you know what this is, Grape?"

"A tiny suitcase?"

"Yes, but do you know what's inside the suitcase?"

"No, but I have to—"

"This, Grape, is a flute case, and do you know what's inside it?"

"Umm…a flute?"

"That's correct, my friend. And guess what that means?"

"You play the flute?"

"I do now! My dad and Principal Whitlock agreed I would be better off if I joined the school band instead of showering with my peers!"

"Oh, cool."

"Cool, indeed! No PE for The Sherm!"

"Cool."

"And hey, Grape?"

"Yeah?"

"Where's Lou?"

I told him, then I ran to PE.

Lou, I wish I played the flute, too.

I got to my locker and took my shoes off, then my pants, then I felt another tap on my shoulder.

"Hello, Grape."

It was Maxwell. He had his PE uniform on already.

"What's your favorite sport?" he said.

The thing is, I was in my underwear, so I really didn't want to talk about sports.

"Um…dodgeball."

He kind of laughed. "No, Grape. I mean a real sport."

"It is a real sport."

He laughed again and put his fingers through his hair. "If you say so," he said. "I'm a football-basketball man myself."

"Oh, cool."

"Never understood the point of dodgeball."

I wanted to explain dodgeball to Maxwell, but then we heard Coach Ruth's whistle.

BREEEP!

"Well, see you out there, Mr. Underwear Dodgeball."

I put my uniform on super fast, then I got my lock out of my backpack.

But the thing is, I couldn't remember my combination.

I took my PE uniform off and stuffed it in my backpack, then I put my clothes back on and ran outside.

Coach Ruth stood there with a clipboard. "Lining you up alphabetically. Five rows," he said. "When your name's called, get in line. Remember your position. Tomorrow, expect you there. Three simple rules, people. Rule one—"

Then he saw me through his sunglasses and stopped talking about rule one.

"Where the heck's your uni?" he said.

"Huh?"

"Your uniform!"

"Um…in my backpack, sir!"

"What the—"

"I forgot my combination, sir!"

He shook his head. "*This* is why I stressed it! Memorize combos!"

I wanted to tell him I was super bad at math.

"Park it there," he said, and pointed to a bench.

So that's what I did. I parked it.

Everyone did jumping jacks and ran around the field, and at the end of class Coach Ruth said he has to give me an absence.

I said okay.

"And one less day conditioning for six-minute run," he said.

I said okay again.

At lunch I waited in line for my tray of milk and Tater Tots and chicken strips and Jell-O, then I looked for Clair, but Clair was eating with Maxwell, so I sat with Sherman. We talked about his flute and he asked me about my bar mitzvah, then the bell rang for free time, but I was still eating, then I finished eating and put my tray back in the tray-stacking place, then I went to the basketball court but the game had started already, so I went to the tetherball court, but there was a super long line, so I went back to the lunch table and sat with Sherman until Sherman said, "Shall we walk around?"

So that's what we did.

We walked around.

The bell rang, and I ran to double-period math.

It was super boring.

Your best friend,
Grape

Rabbi Len is Going to Be My Tutor, and My Dad Gets Sailing-Mad

September 8, 1976

Dear Lou,

Today my mom picked me up for after-school Hebrew tutoring.

"Here is Mentos," she said, then she took my hand and put it on her belly. "Feel, the baby move."

I felt the baby move.

It was super weird.

"*Todo bien*, Grape. Don't be scared."

"Okay."

Then my mom said something that did scare me.

"Is a new tutor, Grape."

I went into the study room and a lady stood up and put her hand out.

"*Ma shimcha? Shmi* Esther."

"Um...*shmi E-nahv*," I said.

"*Ma shlomcha?*"

"Um..."

"*Ma shlomcha, E-nahv.*"

"Um...*Merkavah.*"

"Chariot?"

She said a few more words in Hebrew, then she said, "Wait here," in English.

So that's what I did.

I waited.

And the spiders started spinning.

Hey, Grape.

Yeah?

The bikini magazine!

"But…Esther!"

Hurry!

I pulled my chair over to the bookshelf, then I stood on it, then I pulled the big red book out, and the magazine was still there! I put the book back, then I pulled my chair back, then I looked at the bikini ladies, then I heard Esther yelling in Hebrew, and the thing is, her voice was coming closer.

I threw the magazine under the table.

Rabbi Len walked in with Esther. She pointed at me and said something in Hebrew and shook her head.

It was like being called to the kitchen table.

"*Toda*," the rabbi said, and Esther left.

"Hi, Grape."

"Hi."

"Esther says you haven't made much progress."

"Um…"

"What have you been doing all this time?"

I didn't know what to say. The thing is, I didn't want to get Aaron in trouble, but I also didn't want to lie to Rabbi Len.

I just stared at him.

"You know, this bar mitzvah is very important to your mom and dad. You have relatives coming from Argentina."

I started to cry.

"You can tell me the truth, Grape. This isn't like school. You don't get a grade."

"Will Aaron get in trouble?"

"Aaron quit, so, no, he won't get in trouble."

"Did he quit because of Sasha?"

"Who's Sasha?"

I told Rabbi Len about Sasha and how Aaron was super sad and ran his hand through his hair and said her name over and over, and the rabbi laughed a little, then he said, "That's all fine, but what did you do the rest of the time?"

I crawled under the table and showed him the magazine. He shook his head.

"Grape, when your mom picks you up, I want both of you in my office."

The thing is, my mom didn't pick me up. My mom and dad did, and my dad had his floppy hat and super-white sunscreen on.

"Is surprise sailing!" my dad said.

I also had a surprise.

"Um…the rabbi wants to talk to you," I said.

Rabbi Len met us in the waiting room.

"Rabbi," my dad said, "is a good day to be alive! Come sailing with us! ¿Angélica, *tienes* sunscreen *para el* rabbi?"

But Rabbi Len didn't want to go sailing. "Grape," he said, "tell your parents what happened."

So I did.

"*Dios mío,*" my mom said.

My dad took his glasses off and rubbed his eyes, then he put his glasses back on.

"I am sorry, Rabbi," he said.

"No. *I* am sorry," Rabbi Len said. "Aaron was our responsibility."

"*Qué cosa,*" my mom said. "*Pobrecito* rabbi."

"Mr. and Mrs. Borokovich, given Grape's setback, we should move his bar mitzvah to later in the year."

"Rabbi," my dad said, "is impossible!"

"Grape," the rabbi said, "there's a chair in the hallway. Wait there."

So that's what I did. I waited in the hallway.

I could hear my dad yelling *is impossible, plane tickets, the baby* and my mom saying *¡es increíble!*, and Esther walked by and shook her head at me, then I heard *one strategy we might try* and *Sears* and my dad saying, *thank you, Rabbi,* then my mom and dad walked out and Rabbi Len called my name.

I carried my chair in.

"What are you doing, Grape?"

I told him about the last official meeting with Mrs. C.

"But there are plenty of chairs in here."

"Oh, sorry."

"First, I want to apologize again. Aaron was our responsibility."

Lou, the rabbi apologized to me!

But he was also kind of mad. "Grape," he said, "you should have told someone what was happening."

"I'm sorry."

"Do you realize how important your bar mitzvah is to your parents?"

I told him I did.

"The whole purpose of tutoring is to improve your Hebrew, but instead, you looked at car magazines! What were you thinking?"

I told him I wasn't thinking. The spiders were.

"What spiders?"

I told him.

He stroked his invisible beard. "It must be tough having spiders," he said.

"It is."

"Well, spiders or not, it seems we can't move your bar mitzvah."

"I'm sorry."

"But I do have an idea."

"Okay."

"It's unconventional, but it might work."

"Do you want me to write a trouble book?"

"A what?"

I told him.

"No, Grape."

He opened a drawer and took out a tiny cassette deck. "This," he said, "is our solution."

Lou, I didn't understand.

"I'm going to record a few lines of your Torah portion, and you're going to listen to it as much as possible."

"Okay."

"Grape, I need you to memorize these lines. Do you think you can do that?"

I told him I could.

"After that, we'll look at the Hebrew and you'll put two and two together."

"Okay."

"Then I'll add more."

"Will I still have tutoring?"

He kind of sat back in his chair. "Yes," he said, "but I'm taking over. Aaron was our responsibility."

Lou, Rabbi Len is going to be my tutor!

"Do you realize how important this is to your mom and dad?" he said.

I wished he would stop saying that.

"Yes," I said.

We just sat there.

"Rabbi?" I said.

"Yes, Grape."

"Can Sherman do my bar mitzvah instead?"

"Who's Sherman?"

I told him.

"No, Grape, but I like your creativity."

"You're welcome," I said.

"Now, let me show you how this works."

He pressed two buttons, and then he kind of sang a bunch of Hebrew words, then he took the cassette out and told me to give it to my mom and dad.

We were super late for sailing, and we still had to go to Sears to buy the tiny cassette deck. We parked, then my dad got out and slammed the car door. My mom shuffled through her purse and took out a Mentos.

"Mom?"

She took a deep breath.

"*¿Sí*, Grape?"

"We still have to ask Betsy to help with the book cover."

"*¿Qué* book cover?"

"The science book for Mr. Frasier's class! Remember I told you?"

"*Pobrecita* Betsy, *pobrecito* Javier."

When my dad got back he slammed the car door again, then he opened the tiny cassette deck and put the batteries in, then he put the cassette in and said I have to listen the whole way to Marina del Sol.

We only sailed a little.

My dad kept asking my mom if she was okay.

"*Sí*, Javier," she said.

"*¿Puedes manejar?*" he said.

"*Sí*, Javier."

My mom took the tiller and my dad lifted the front sail, then the back sail, and the thing is, he didn't ask me to help or to check if water was spitting from the tailpipe thing. Then he turned the motor off and took the tiller.

It was super quiet.

The wind was even and strong.

Then all of a sudden my mom pointed and kind of yelled, "*¡Mira eso!*"

Lou, the sun was going into the ocean like a golden ball.

It was super pretty.

Then I did something.

I walked across the cockpit and stood in front of my dad and said, "I'm sorry about the Hebrew."

He looked at me. I could tell he was still mad, but he was sailing-mad.

"Take the tiller and point the boat into the wind," he said. "Is time to take the sails down."

He let me steer the whole way back.

Your best friend,
Grape

My Birthday Idea

September 13, 1976

Dear Lou,

I'm having a Don Quixote birthday party.

I asked mom to buy invitations, but my dad said I should make my own invitations because I'm becoming a young man now.

So that's what I did, and since I'm only inviting Sherman and Clair and your mom, it was super easy.

I started with Sherman.

Dear Sherman,

I'm having a Don Quixote dress-up birthday party.

It starts at 12:30.

Grape

Then I wrote one for your mom.

Dear Betsy,

I'm having a Don Quixote dress-up birthday party.

It starts at 12:30.

You can wear your Jack Lalanne outfit if you want.

Grape

Then I wrote one for Clair, but it wasn't a Don Quixote invitation. It was an Emily Dickinson one.

Dear Clair,

I'm Grape—to be—Thirteen

Inviting Clair—I mean

At Thirty—minutes

Past—Twelve

To my Don Quixote

Dress-up—Party!

Grape

Lou, I'd never written invitations before. It was super fun!
Then I did something else I'd never done before.

I made my own lunch.

It was Sherman's idea. The thing is, since Sherman brings
his lunch, he doesn't have to wait in the cafeteria line like I
do, so I end up eating my Tater Tots and chicken strips and
Jell-O and listening to him talk about his flute and not having
PE, then I have to put my tray back in the tray-stacking place,
and by that time the bell has already rung.

Then one day Sherman said, "Hey, Grape, why don't you
bring a lunch from home? That way we'll have more time to
walk around."

I asked my mom, and she said yes, but my dad said I
should make my own lunch because I'm becoming a young
man now.

And the thing is, he was super serious.

Lou, I think my dad's getting nervous. When he's happy
he talks about sailing and the baby, and he sings and says,
"Is good to be alive!" and streaks on the sailboat. When he's
serious he talks about my bar mitzvah and his voice gets kind
of quiet and he takes his glasses off and rubs his eyes.

I brought my lunch to school, and Sherman was right! I
finished before the bell rang. Sherman talked about his flute,
then I gave him his invitation.

"It's a Don Quixote party," I said.

"A what?"

"It's a book about a super old guy who thinks he's a
knight."

"Never heard of it," Sherman said.

I couldn't believe it. I knew something Sherman didn't
know.

"But I tell you what, Grape. I'm honored to be invited. I'll
research the title and come prepared."

"Cool."

Then the bell rang, but I didn't walk around with Sherman.
The thing is, I saw Clair walking into Mr. Conway's room.

"I need help," I said.

"We all do," Sherman said, "especially that Bully Jim character."

"In English," I said.

"I thought that's your best subject."

"Yeah, but it's, um…"

"It's that Clair girl, right?"

Lou, Sherman is super smart.

"I'm going to invite her to my birthday," I said.

"You have my blessings, Grape."

Sherman of the Blessed Flute.

Mr. Conway had his feet on his desk and he was reading a newspaper.

"Hi, Grape," he said, "what's up?"

"Oh, um, *Don Quixote.*"

"You want to work on your essay or your poster?"

"Yes," I said.

"You mean both?"

"Yes."

Then I heard, "Hi, Grape!"

"Oh, hi, Clair! What are you doing here?"

"Working on my poster. Do you want to see it?"

"Okay."

I walked over to her desk. Her poster was super dramatic.

"I wanted to do the part when he attacks the monks," she said, "but my mom made me do the book burning instead."

"Cool!"

"What about you?"

"My mom's going to have a baby," I said.

"You told me that already, Grape."

"Oh, sorry."

"I mean your poster."

"Oh, um…I'm drawing Evel Knievel riding next to Don Quixote."

"That's funny, Grape!"

"Thank you, Clair!"

I ran and got my poster and unrolled it and put it next to hers.

"Oh, I'm sorry," she said, "someone's sitting there."

The thing is, no one was sitting there.

Then the door opened. It was Maxwell.

He got his poster and sat next to Clair.

I just stood there.

"Hello, Grape," Maxwell said.

"Hi."

"What are you doing here?"

"Um…my poster."

"What are you representing?"

I told him.

"I don't get it," he said.

"Because Evel Knievel is like Don Quixote," I said.

"It's funny," Clair said.

"Hmm…I'm having a hard time seeing it," Maxwell said, then he pinched his lips together and kind of breathed through his nose.

I moved to another table and pretended to work on my poster, and after a while the bell rang.

I threw Clair's invitation in the trash and ran to PE.

Today was basketball.

I was on the team against Bully Jim and Maxwell.

The thing is, Bully Jim isn't good at shooting, but he's super good at rebounding. Maxwell *is* super good at shooting, so every time Bully Jim rebounded, Maxwell said, "Ball! Ball, big man!" then Bully Jim passed the ball, then Maxwell dribbled super fancy and announced all the plays, like, "Big man rebounds, passes to Maxwell, Maxwell flashes by Grape and scoops in for a lefty layup."

I started to get asthma.

"Time out!" I said.

But nobody timed out.

"Grape walks off the court in defeat," Maxwell said, "and hey, big man, pass the ball, big man!'"

I told Coach Ruth I needed to get my asthma pill from the nurse.

He looked at me through his sunglasses. "Why didn't you take it before class?" he said.

"I'm only supposed to take it when I wheeze."

He shook his head, and the veins in his neck bulged out. "Fine," he said, "get your pill and then park it on the bench."

I said okay.

"How about you take your pill before the six-minute run on Friday? It's all about those six minutes, Grape."

I just stared at him.

"And I have to give you an absence."

Lou, I hate Coach Ruth.

When PE was over I sat at my locker trying to remember my combination, then I felt a tap on my shoulder.

"Hey, Grapeface."

"Hey, Bully Jim."

"Don't call me that."

"Sorry."

"Grapeface, that Maxwell kid is a jerk."

"He's a jerk-off jerk," I said.

Bully Jim laughed. "We should get him," he said.

"Okay."

"We've got to get him," he said again.

"Okay," I said.

We just kind of sat there, then I had an idea.

"Do you want to come to my birthday party?"

"You mean me?" he said.

"It's a Don Quixote birthday."

He just stared.

"He's this super old guy who thinks he's a knight, and the thing is, he gets a super old horse and—"

"You mean a dress-up party?"

"Um…yeah."

"That sounds fun, Grapeface."

Lou, I couldn't believe it.

Bully Jim of the Surprises.

Your best friend,
Grape

My Don Quixote Birthday Party

September 21, 1976

Dear Lou,

My Don Quixote birthday party was yesterday.

I wish you could have been there.

Sherman wore a straw hat and a super big white fluffy shirt with pillows under it and pants with a bunch of holes. "I'm Sancho Panza," he said. "I read several chapters, Grape! Hilarious material! Anyway, I assumed you would want to go as the protagonist, and what better way to celebrate your birth than to be your sidekick?"

I had no idea what he was talking about, but he looked super funny.

Bully Jim wore a black cape and he had a cap gun hanging from his waist like a cowboy in *Movie of the Week*.

Lou, I don't think Bully Jim understands knighthood.

"My gun is loaded with silver bullets, Grapeface. To shoot vampires!"

"Actually," Sherman said, "it's werewolves who die from silver bullets. You'll want a wooden stake through the heart for vampires."

Bully Jim just looked at him.

We ate pizza, then my mom and dad surprised me with an Evel Knievel cake, then we opened the presents.

Sherman got me a recorder.

"It's like a flute," he said, "but more primitive."

"Oh…um…thanks."

"You're very welcome, Grape."

Bully Jim gave me a yo-yo.

"That's for your birthday," he said.

Your mom gave me a fancy exercise tank top.

"It captures sweat!" she said.

My mom and dad gave me a new Elton John watch.

After cake, Sherman asked if I wanted to practice my recorder.

I told him I didn't.

Bully Jim asked if there was more cake.

My mom said there was.

We kind of just sat there, then I had an idea.

"Let's go to the park," I said.

Bully Jim said, "Sure, Grapeface," and Sherman said, "Your wish is my command. It is your turn around the sun, after all!"

Lou, it was super cool. Heidi said, "Happy birthday, kid," and Rusty said, "Happy B-day, man," then we heard the ice cream truck, then Heidi got on her bike and came back with five Bomb Pops. But the thing is, it was super hot and the Bomb Pops kept melting on our hands, so we sat on the cement slab licking our fingers. Then Rusty played Black Sabbath on the boom box and told us to listen to the lyrics, then Bully Jim said, "Hell, yes!" and did air guitar, then Sherman said he couldn't understand what the singer guy was saying, then Rusty said he needs to open his ears, then Sherman said his ears were open, then Rusty said, "Whatever, man," and lit a cigarette and blew smoke rings, then Sherman said, "Oh, I see!" Then Bully Jim asked if he could ride Rusty's bike, and Rusty said okay, then I asked Heidi if I could ride her bike, then she said okay, then I rode down the gully with Bully Jim and showed him how I could do a wheelie, then Bully Jim showed me how he could do a wheelie, and when we got back, Heidi was teaching Sherman how to stand on a skateboard. It was super funny because he still had his Sancho Panza costume on, then I realized I still had my Don Quixote costume on and Bully Jim still had his cape on, then Heidi said she had to leave or her new parents will kill her, then we all walked back to my house and watched *Gilligan's Island.*

Your best friend,
Grape

The Long Sail, Over

September 30, 1976

Dear Lou,

My life is brutal busy.

I have regular school with Mr. Conway and Mr. Frasier and Coach Ruth and my math teacher, then I have Hebrew school with Rabbi Len and pop-a-wheelie school with Heidi, and now I have another kind of school.

Sailing school, with *Capitán* Javier.

Tonight we had a super-important lesson.

It was about The Long Sail.

The thing is, usually when my dad comes home from work, he goes straight to his room and gets his robe and slippers on because he's super ready for dinner, but tonight he yelled, "Grape, to the kitchen!" and I thought I was in trouble.

He was standing with his briefcase and a roll of blueprints, but the thing is, it didn't smell like ammonia.

Lou, it wasn't blueprints. It was a map of the ocean.

He unrolled the map and used our cups to hold down the corners. There were blue squiggly lines and red squiggly lines, then he said something about currents and my mom said, "*¡Por favor,* Javier, *los vasos!*" and my dad said, "*Es importante,* Angélica. Is for The Long Sail!"

"*¿Qué* Long Sail?" my mom said.

"*¡Esto,* Angélica, *mira!*" He took an architect pencil out of his shirt pocket and made a little X on the map. "Here is Marina del Sol," he said, and then he made another little X on the map, "and this is how far we have sailed."

"*Muy bien,* Javier," my mom said, "*y ahora—*"

"But *here*," he said, "is where we go for The Long Sail," then he made another little X on the map.

"*Muy bien*," my mom said, "*y ahora vamos a comer—*"

"Five or six hours!" my dad said.

"*Muy bien*, Javier, five or six hours," my mom said.

"But is dangerous," he said.

We just looked at him.

"*Muy bien*, is dangerous," my mom said, "*y ahora vamos a comer. El bebé* is hungry."

But my dad didn't care about the baby.

"Grape," he said, "what is dangerous about The Long Sail?"

"Um…it's long?"

"No! Angélica, what is dangerous about The Long Sail?"

My mom took her apron off and sat down and slapped the table. "*¡Dios mío*, Javier! I don't know! *Dime, ¿que tiene de peligroso el* Long Sail?"

My dad closed the kitchen doors.

"Is the tankers!" he said. He pointed at the map. "Look! Is the shipping lane of the tankers!"

"*¿Qué son los* tankers?" my mom said.

Lou, tankers are gigantic boats as wide as a freeway and tall as a building, and they look like they're going super slow but they're really going super fast, and they have their own lanes, and the thing is, we have to cross those lanes on The Long Sail.

"And if we see the tanker," my dad said, "we yell, *Tanker!* and we slow down or we tack or we change the angle. Let me put it this way…"

It was super boring, like math.

Then it wasn't.

"The tanker moves too fast to stop or turn around," my dad said. "Is like a train on the water, and if there is a collision, who will win, *mi hijo?*"

"The tanker!" I said.

"Angélica, who will win?"

"*Nadie*, Javier. Because before the tanker, *voy a morir de hambre.*"

Lou, my mom was super hungry.

"Is why we learn angles and we tack and call out *Tanker!*" my dad said. "Now we eat dinner, and after, we learn how to use the radio."

My mom put her apron on super fast, then she brought our food and my dad talked about tankers and collisions and my mom ate super fast, then she made tea and said the baby was happy now, then my dad told me to rinse the dishes because I'm becoming a young man, so that's what I did, then he said how important it was for us to learn how to use the radio.

The thing is, the radio was in the boat, so we pretended the phone was the radio.

I told him I knew how to use a phone.

"Is different, *mi hijo*! Only one person can talk, then you say *over!*"

"*¿Como la policía en Movie of the Week?*" my mom said.

"*Sí*, and when you're done you have to say, *Over and out.*"

"Cool," I said.

"And if an emergency, you say, *Mayday! Over!*"

"Cool," I said.

"Grape, say, *Mayday! Over!*"

"*Mayday! Over!*" I said.

"Angélica!"

"*Mayday!*" my mom said.

"*Over!*" my dad said.

"*Over!*" my mom said.

"*¡Muy bien!* Tonight we practice our *overs* and *mañana* we practice on the boat, and soon The Long Sail!"

"*Dios mío*," my mom said.

"*Dios mío, over!*" my dad said.

"Can I go to my room now?" I said.

"*Over!*" my dad said.

"Can I go to my room now, *over?*"

"But is dessert, Grape," my mom said.

My dad looked at her.

"Is dessert, *over*," my mom said.

I just shook my head.

In the morning my dad had his floppy hat and super-white sunscreen on, and my mom wore her red visor and put sunscreen all over my face and arms, then we drove to Marina del Sol.

Lou, my dad was right. The radio wasn't like a phone. It was like a CB.

My dad went first. "Channel 63, this is *Spray*. Over."

"Come in, *Spray*. Over."

"Departing Marina del Sol, over."

"Copy that. Over."

"Over and out," my dad said.

My mom was next.

"Channel 63. Is Angélica. Over!"

"No!" my dad said. "*¡No digas tu nombre!* Say the name of the boat!"

"Is *Spray*," she said.

"*Over*, Mom!"

"Channel 63," my mom said, "is *Spray*. OVER!"

"Copy that," the radio guy said. "Over."

"*¡Muy bien!*" my dad said.

"*¡Qué cosa!*" my mom said. "*¿Porque no tenien telefonos?*"

"Is one-way radio!" my dad said.

"*Spray*, are you still there?" the radio guy said. "Over."

"*¡Angélica, di algo!*"

"*Sí*," my mom said, "*todo bien.* Over!"

"What's that? Over."

"*¡Inglés!*" my dad said.

"Is okay," my mom said, "Over and out!" and then she

just let go of the radio mouthpiece thing, and it hung there. "*¡No me gusta el radio,* Javier!" she said, then he helped her up the companionway.

"Grape, *practica con el radio,*" my dad said.

Lou, my dad said I did great, but the radio guy said we only need to check in once.

Your best friend,
Grape

The Second Worst Day of My Life

October 7, 1976

Dear Lou,

Today was the second worst day of my life.

During lunch I saw Clair and Maxwell holding hands.

So did Sherman.

"Well, Grape," he said, "I'm sorry to see that."

"Me too."

"You can't win them all."

"I know."

"But you have to hand it to that Maxwell kid. He has quite the hair, like a lion's."

"You wanna walk around?" I said.

"Sorry, Grape. Flute practice. First recital coming up."

So I walked around by myself.

I walked past the basketball courts and around the field and I saw three turkey vultures. Then I walked to the tetherball courts, but the line was super long, then I saw Mr. Frasier and said I'm sorry I haven't done my book cover yet, but he said he didn't care because Admin never spends on students and maybe it's better to let the books rot. Then I walked to my book locker and spun the combination, then I opened my locker and closed it again and opened it again, then I went to the bathroom and looked in the mirror and tried to make my hair look like a lion's. And then since I didn't want to do stupid PE, I ran around the track to give myself asthma, but it didn't work, so I went to the edge of the field and pulled some weeds and sniffed them, then the bell rang, but instead of going to the locker room and changing I went straight to Coach Ruth and said I have asthma.

He looked at me through his sunglasses. "I don't hear you wheezing," he said.

"Yeah, but—"

"Dress out, Grape."

"Yeah, but—"

"Dress out, Grape. Or get an absence. Absence affects grade. My policy is—"

"Okay."

"Okay, what?"

"Okay, I'll get a stupid absence."

He looked at me for a long time. "I tell you what," he said, "I'll do you one better."

Lou, Principal Whitlock is kind of nice and kind of mean.

He switches around a lot.

Whitlock of the Switching Countenance.

And the thing is, his office switches, too. There are fancy certificates with his name on them like a normal principal's office, but he also has an Evel Knievel poster!

"I'm surprised it's taken so long for you to visit," he said. "Your reputation precedes you."

"Thank you," I said.

"You want to tell me what happened with Coach Ruth."

The thing is, I wasn't listening.

I was looking at the Evel Knievel poster.

He's on his motorcycle, and he's wearing his Evel Knievel jacket and pants and helmet, and he's super high in the clouds, like he's jumping over the Earth.

"I see you like Evel," Principal Whitlock said.

"I have an Evel Knievel bike and an Evel Knievel jacket and helmet, and I can pop a wheelie but not uphill yet, but my friend Heidi is teaching me, and I can jump four cans."

"That's impressive, Grape."

"Thank you."

"You know, everyone talks about the Snake River Canyon

jump and that silly rocket and all that, but my favorite is the fourteen Greyhound buses. October 1975. You want to know why?"

"Okay."

"Because he was coming off a failure, Grape. A terrible failure."

"He was?"

"Yep, in England. Eighty thousand people, and Evel flips his Harley and his Harley practically chases him as he bounces off the cement."

"Really?"

"He manages to stand himself up, then he asks for the microphone and says that's it, he's done jumping."

"But—"

"That's right, Grape. A few months later, there he is, clearing fourteen Greyhounds!"

Lou, Principal Whitlock's cool.

Then he did the switching thing, and he wasn't cool anymore.

He waved Coach Ruth's disobedience sheet and pointed at it and kind of yelled. "This!" he said, "tell me about this!"

So I did.

"Well, it's unacceptable, no good, reflects badly on you. Your reputation precedes you, and you arrived a step away from Riverwash!"

Then he switched again.

"Can I read you something, Grape?"

"Um…okay."

He opened a filing cabinet and pulled out a folder.

"I have a list of my favorite quotes here," he said. "I keep them handy in moments of crisis."

"Cool."

"So that's what I'm doing now. I'm finding a quote. Do you understand?"

"Yes."

"I've collected over a thousand quotes!"

"Um...cool."

"All right...here goes." Principal Whitlock cleared his throat. "'You are the master of your own ship, pal. There are lots of people who fall into troubled waters and don't have the guts or the knowledge or the ability to make it to shore. They have nobody to blame but themselves.'"

Lou, I didn't know what ship he was talking about.

We just sat there.

"Well, what do you think?" he said.

"Cool," I said.

"Let me read it again."

So that's what he did. He read it again.

"Who do you think said those words, Grape?"

I told him I didn't know.

He pointed at the poster.

"Really?" I said.

"Yup! How about I make you a copy?"

"Okay."

"Be right back," he said.

He left me alone in his office, then he came back with a copy of the quote.

"Grape," he said, "promise me you'll put these words somewhere safe."

"Um...okay."

"And think about them when you're struggling. After all, they're from the horse's mouth!"

Lou, I didn't know what horse he was talking about.

"I should probably send you home," he said, "send a message and all of that, but Coach Ruth, well, he's pretty one-dimensional. Gosh, I don't know..." He paced behind his desk like a lawyer in *Movie of the Week*, then he said, "Gosh, sometimes I hate this job, but I'm the decider!"

He looked at the poster and put his palms up like he was asking Evel Knievel what to do.

My mom picked me up and I told her about stupid Coach Ruth and my asthma and she said, "Grape, is okay. Here is Mentos."

I told her I didn't want a Mentos.

"I want a haircut," I said.

My mom looked at me. The thing is, I'd never asked for a haircut before.

"Okay, *mañana* I take you for a haircut."

"No, Mom. Today!"

"Is the oil change today."

"MOM!"

"*¿Por qué es tan importante?*"

"Because it stupid is!" I said.

My mom left me at the haircut place and told me she'd pick me up after the oil change.

The haircut lady was super nice. She even liked my name.

"I've been cutting hair a long time, sweetie, and that's the best name I've ever heard."

"Thank you."

"You're very welcome. Now, how do you want your hair, just shorter on the sides, and—"

"Like a wave with little waves in it," I said.

"I'm not sure what you mean, sweetie."

"Like a lion's."

"Oh, dear…can you describe it more?"

I told her I couldn't.

"Well, okay, then, I have another idea." She got a magazine from the counter. "Look through here and point to the kind of cut you want."

I looked, then I pointed.

"That's a feathered cut, sweetie."

"That's what I want," I said. "I want feathered."

"Problem is your hair doesn't lie out like that. It's naturally wavy."

I didn't say anything.

She turned the pages. "How about something like this?" she said.

It was the same haircut I have now, but shorter.

"No. I want feathered."

"Your hair won't feather, sweetie, that's what I'm trying to tell you."

I just sat there.

Then the haircut lady said something.

"What's her name?"

"Who?"

"The girl you like."

Lou, I couldn't believe it. She was like Dr. Vecchi.

"Um...Clair."

"And Clair likes someone else?"

"Yes."

"And he has feathered hair?"

"Yes."

"Well, sweetie, I know how you feel."

"You do?"

"I changed my hairstyle for my first husband, and then again when..."

She talked a super long time about her first husband and her boyfriend and her kids, but she wasn't nervous like your mom. Then she said, "I tell you what, let's find you something fresh, something Clair will love."

"Okay."

"You study that magazine until something strikes you."

So that's what I did. I studied the magazine, and something struck me.

"That's a spiky shag, sweetie. Rock star, heavy metal type."

"Like Black Sabbath?"

She laughed. "You got it!"

"Cool."

"Are you sure your mom will be okay with it?"

"Yes."

"Maybe we should wait to see what she thinks?"

"No."

When she was done, she asked if I wanted a little gel.

"Okay."

"This will spike it a bit, but if you want to keep it that way you'll have to buy a bottle."

"Cool," I said.

"I just hope your mom's okay with it."

When my mom got back from the oil change, she said, "*¡Dios mío!*" three times, and she didn't buy the gel.

When I got home I rode straight to the park.

But the thing is, Heidi wasn't there. It was just Rusty sitting on a skateboard and smoking a cigarette.

I took my helmet off.

"Cool hair," Rusty said.

"The haircut lady said I look like Black Sabbath."

"Right on," he said.

"Where's Heidi?"

"I don't know, man."

I popped a few wheelies, then I asked Rusty if he wanted to set up the ramps, but he said it was a skating day for him, so he rode his skateboard and I popped a few more wheelies, then I practiced skidding, then I took a break and waited for Heidi, then I popped a few more wheelies, then I got thirsty and rode to the playground and drank some water, then I turned around. The sandbox was empty.

Hey, Grape?

"Yeah?"

Do you see that clay turtle?

"Yes."

Remember what Heidi said about that turtle?

"No."

She said a pro could take off from the edge of the sandbox and jump it. No ramp or anything.

"Oh yeah."

You need to jump the turtle, Grape.

"But I'm not a pro."

Yeah, but it will be the coolest thing ever.

"It will?"

Yes!

"But I might crash."

That never stopped Evel.

Lou, it was true.

Be like Evel, Grape.

"Okay."

I rode my bike to the edge of the sandbox the way Evel rides to the end of his ramps.

Good! Now ride out far enough to pick up speed.

So that's what I did.

Ladies and Gentlemen, I give you Grape! The first to jump the sandbox turtle!

I pedaled super hard, then I heard a voice.

But it wasn't the spiders.

It was Heidi.

"Kid! Kid! What are you—"

I pulled up on the bike and tried to make myself light.

But I didn't make myself light.

My front tire bumped the turtle's head, then I flipped over my handlebars and my helmet hit the shell, then I landed on the sand, then my bike landed on me.

"Kid! Kid! What are you doing? Are you crazy?"

"I…um…it's okay, sweetie. Look through the magazine."

"What?"

"*Clair of the Feathered Texas.*"

"Kid, you're not making any sense! You crashed something brutal!"

Heidi took my helmet off, then she helped me to the drinking fountain and washed the sand and blood off my face.

"Kid, your chin's messed up."

"It hurts."

"I think you'll need stitches."

"Okay."

"Can you ride?"

"I think so."

"Pedal a few and see."

But I couldn't pedal a few. When I sat on my bike my nut sack hurt something brutal.

"I better push it," I said.

"How far do you live, kid?"

"California," I said.

"No, kid. How long does it take you to ride home?"

"Soon," I said.

Heidi just looked at me. "You stay right here. Don't move!"

"Okay."

When she came back she didn't have her bike.

"I'm going to push it home with you, kid," she said.

So that's what she did. She pushed my bike home with me. On the way, she asked me what day it was and I told her, then she asked me my name and I told her, then she said, "I think you're back, but you crashed something brutal. What were you thinking?"

I told her I wasn't thinking.

"Is that why you got that haircut?"

"What haircut?"

Then something weird happened. A car drove by, then it backed up, then the window rolled down and a man with a headband and sunglasses looked at us, then your mom kind of leaned over the man and asked me if I was okay.

"Yes," I said.

"Are you sure?"

"Yes," I said.

"Who's that?" she said.

"I'm Heidi," Heidi said. "He crashed something brutal."

They drove away.

"That's Betsy," I said, "Lou's mom."

"Who's Lou?"

I told her about the court and how your mom is nervous.

"Everyone's nervous, kid."

When we got to my house, Heidi knocked.

"Who is it?" my mom said.

"It's me, Mom."

My mom opened the door and said, "*Dios mío*, Grape, *¿qué pasó?*"

"He crashed something brutal," Heidi said.

My mom pointed at Heidi. "*¿Y quien es ella?*" she said.

"This is Heidi. She helped me because of the turtle."

"*¿Qué* turtle?" my mom said.

"I think he should go to the hospital," Heidi said.

"*¡Dios mío!*" my mom said.

"All right, kid," Heidi said, "I better go."

"Okay. Thanks, Heidi."

"Feel better. Love you, kid."

My mom kind of looked at Heidi.

Lou, I got six stitches on my chin, then the doctor asked me a bunch of questions and made me follow his finger back and forth with my eyes.

"He's likely concussed," he said.

"*Qué cosa*," my mom said.

"No physical activity for two weeks, then have him checked again. If he's dizzy or starts vomiting, get him to a hospital right away."

"Does this mean I can skip PE?" I said.

"Absolutely," the doctor said.

"Because, the thing is, Coach Ruth is super official, and all he talks about is the six-minute run, and—"

The doctor told me to get some rest.

On the ride home my mom asked about Heidi.

"She's super cool, Mom. She taught me how to pop a wheelie."

"*¡Es vieja!*"

"She's seventeen."

"*¿Qué hace?*"

"She's in high school."

"*Muy vieja*," she said again.

"She's my new best friend, Mom!"

"Lou is your best friend, Grape."

"LOU ISN'T HERE!"

My mom took a deep breath. "Is right. Lou isn't here."

Then I asked about your mom and the guy with the headband.

"Betsy *tiene novio*," she said.

Lou, your mom has a boyfriend.

Your best friend,

Grape

The Frog

October 14, 1976

Dear Lou,

At school all I did is explain my stitches and answer the same question over and over again.

"Hey, Grape, what did you do to your hair?"

"A concussion," I said.

The thing is, Coach Ruth didn't care about my hair or my concussion. "Too bad," he said, "you'll have to catch up on conditioning. It's all about the six-minute run."

I just stared at him.

"And you still have to dress out. Every day, Grape."

So that's what I did. I dressed out, and when I came back he handed me a book about Presidential Fitness and told me to read it.

But I didn't read it. Instead, I watched flag football.

And guess who played quarterback?

Maxwell.

And guess who was on Maxwell's team?

Bully Jim!

On the first play, Maxwell passed to Bully Jim, but he dropped it, then Maxwell said, "Soft hands, big man! This isn't woodshop!" and Bully Jim kind of looked at him, then Maxwell said, "How about you just snap the ball and throw a block from now on?"

So that's what Bully Jim did.

"Ready, set, hike!" Maxwell said.

Bully Jim snapped the ball, then he turned around and knocked Maxwell over.

"What the hell?" Maxwell said.

Bully Jim stood over him. "I thought you said to block," he said.

"The other team, stupid!"

I thought Bully Jim would kill him.

But he didn't. He just walked away.

It was super cool.

On the way to lunch I stopped at the drinking fountain and felt a tap on my shoulder.

"Cool stitches, Grapeface."

"Thanks, Bully Jim."

"Don't call me that."

"Okay. Um…"

"Jimmy. Call me Jimmy."

"Okay."

"It's just that I don't want to go to Riverwash."

Lou, I couldn't believe it!

"Did you have to write a trouble book?"

"What are you talking about, Grapeface?"

"Um…nothing. But hey, that Maxwell kid…you would kill him in dodgeball."

"Thanks, Grapeface. You're right. I would. And if it wasn't for Riverwash, I would kick his butt."

"Me, too!" I said.

"I say we get him."

"Okay!"

"Let's get him, Grapeface."

"Okay!"

"We just have to wait for the right time."

A few days later we were in Mr. Frasier's class and it was the right time.

The frogs were on metal trays, one for each station. Mr. Frasier moved behind the skeleton.

"Mr. Bones says no funny stuff or I'll have to send you to the warden, aka Admin!"

Sherman laughed like crazy.

"Now take over, Mr. Kaufman!"

Lou, Sherman was like the teacher's aide. He showed us how to hold the scalpel, then he told us to stab the anus first, then cut across the abdomen, then open the flaps of the abdomen, then pin the flaps down. "And after you stab the anus and pin the flaps," he said, "identify the major organs. These would be the liver, heart, lungs, and bladder. Note these on your anatomy worksheet. I will be making my rounds in the event that you need help," he said. "Just remember, start with the anus."

Lou, Sherman really liked saying *anus*.

"Mr. Bones, may they proceed?" he said.

"Proceed!" Mr. Bones said.

Bully Jim grabbed the scalpel, but he didn't start with the anus. Instead, he cut the frog's legs off.

"No!" Sherman said. "What are you doing? The slice goes from the anus to the head. The *anus!*"

"Oh, sorry," Bully Jim said.

"There's no need to identify the legs! They're already exposed, and they're *not* a major organ! I don't see the legs on the anatomy worksheet! Didn't you hear a word I said?"

Bully Jim kind of stared at him, and the thing is, he was holding the scalpel. Sherman left.

Then Bully Jim stabbed the frog in the belly a bunch of times.

"Hey, Grapeface," he said, "want a turn?"

I told him I didn't.

Bully Jim kept stabbing, then he sliced across the belly and the skin kind of flapped open, then he told me to hold the skin while he pinned it down, so that's what I did. We could see the frog's insides, but the thing is, we couldn't identify the major organs because they were all stabbed and bloody, so we just guessed on the worksheet, then Mr. Bones said it was time for cleanup.

"First, dispose of the carcass in the barrel!" Sherman said.

But Bully Jim didn't dispose of the carcass. Instead, he cut the frog's head off and wrapped it in a paper towel.

"Hey, Grapeface," he said. "Open your backpack! Hurry!"

I opened my backpack and he put the frog's head inside.

"Meet you at lunch," he said.

At the lunch table Bully Jim said, "What's up, Grapeface," and I said, "What's up?" then he said, "What's up, Sherman?" and Sherman said, "Why, hello, Bully Jim, nice of you to visit," then Bully Jim said, "Call me Jimmy from now on," then he sat down.

It was super weird. I could tell Sherman wanted Bully Jim to leave, and Bully Jim wanted Sherman to leave, but I also wanted Sherman to leave because, the thing is, I had a frog head in my backpack.

"Hey, Grape," Sherman said, "aren't you going to eat lunch?"

"Um, no, I'm full."

"But you haven't eaten."

"Yeah, but I'm on a diet."

"What? You're skinny as a rail!"

"Yeah, but…um…it's a Jack LaLanne diet."

"Suit yourself," Sherman said.

The bell rang, and Sherman walked away with his flute.

"We need to make a plan, Grapeface," Bully Jim said.

I said okay.

"We need to get Maxwell!"

I said okay again.

We just sat there.

The thing is, Bully Jim is really bad at making plans.

"We could put the frog in his locker," he said.

"But we don't know his combination."

"Oh yeah."

"We could mail it to his house," he said.

"But we don't have his address," I said.

"Oh yeah. Well, his hair is stupid."

"Yeah," I said, "feathered hair is stupid."

"Your hair is cooler, Grapeface."

"Thanks, Jimmy."

"And he always wears dumb shirts!"

"Like a disco guy," I said.

"Yeah, he's a featherhead disco guy!"

"He probably listens to AM music," I said.

"And he thinks he's cool," Bully Jim said, "because he has a girlfriend."

"What girlfriend?" I said. "He doesn't—"

"It's that Clair girl from Texas."

"What Clair girl—"

"Don't be stupid, Grapeface. Everyone knows you like her."

I didn't say anything.

"But she must be a dummy to choose Featherhead," he said.

Lou, I was mad and happy at the same time.

"Featherhead and Dummy probably go to second base," Bully Jim said.

"Yeah, stupid second base!" I said.

"Wait a minute!" Bully Jim said. "Let's put the frog in his lunch!"

"Lunch is over."

"You're right! But we need to get him, Grapeface."

The bell rang.

"Bring it back tomorrow," Bully Jim said.

"Bring what back?"

"The frog head."

"Yeah, but it's gross—"

"When you get home, put it in the freezer."

"Yeah, but—"

"Do you want to get Featherhead or not?"

"I guess."

"As soon as the bus drops you off, head to the freezer, Grapeface. Head to the freezer!"

The thing is, I couldn't head to the freezer.

I had Hebrew tutoring, and today it was super official.

The secretary told me to meet Rabbi Len at the bimah.

Lou, the bimah is the podium in the main part of the temple, and the thing is, the Torah was open.

It was super dramatic.

But I had a frog head in my backpack, and that was also super dramatic.

"Stand here with me, Grape," Rabbi Len said. "I want you to feel what it's going to be like. You can put your backpack over by the wall."

"Um…why?"

"What do you mean *why?*"

I just looked at him.

"Is something wrong?" he said.

"No."

I put my backpack by the wall.

"Grape," he said, "I have a question."

"Okay."

"Why do you think we're doing this?"

"Because of the car magazines."

"No, that's not what I meant."

"Oh, sorry."

"Grape, why are you having a bar mitzvah?"

I just stared at him.

"Grape?"

"Um…I don't know."

I thought I would be in trouble, but the rabbi kind of smiled. "That's an honest answer, Grape. I appreciate it."

"You're welcome," I said.

"Most kids say it's about becoming a young man or their Jewish identity."

"They do?"

"How can you become a man at thirteen?"

"I don't know."

"You can't, Grape."

We just stood there.

"How about this. How about we try to answer that question when your bar mitzvah's over?"

"Okay."

"Now let's talk about your Torah portion. Sound good?"

"Yes."

"You know about the parting of the Red Sea, but let's talk about what happened before."

"Like in *The Ten Commandments?*" I said.

"You mean the movie?"

"I watched it with my mom and Betsy and Lou, and even though it didn't win Best Picture, we still dressed up."

The rabbi laughed. "All right, that's a good enough place to start."

So I started.

"After Moses is born his mom puts him in a river basket because the pharaoh wants to kill all the Hebrew baby boys, but the pharaoh's daughter finds him floating down the river and adopts him, and he's like a prince."

"Good," the rabbi said. "Go on."

"And then Moses finds out he's Hebrew and becomes a slave like all the other Hebrew people, then he hits a guy and has to run away, then God talks to him from a bush and tells him he has to go back and tell the pharaoh *LET MY PEOPLE GO!* It's super dramatic."

"All right," the rabbi said, "but keep in mind that—"

"The thing is, Moses doesn't want to talk to the pharaoh, but God tells him he has to, so Moses talks to the pharaoh, and the pharaoh says no way, then God tells Moses to tell the pharaoh that if he doesn't *LET MY PEOPLE GO!* he'll start sending plagues, but the pharaoh doesn't believe him!"

"So, why do you think Moses doesn't want to talk with—"

"The first plague is super dramatic. The river turns into blood, but the pharaoh doesn't care, and then there's another one with grasshoppers and storms, and hailstorms and—"

"Don't forget the frogs, Grape."

"What frogs?"

"The second plague. God sends thousands of frogs into the city."

"Oh yeah," I said.

"Go on," the rabbi said.

"For the last plague, God tells Moses to tell the Hebrew people to put lamb's blood on their doors because, the thing is, he's going to kill the oldest boy in all the Egyptian families, but he'll skip over the houses with blood."

"That's right, Grape."

"So that's what he does," I said. "God even kills the pharaoh's son."

"That's right."

"It's super sad."

"It is."

We just kind of sat there.

"Go on."

"Pharaoh says Moses can LET MY PEOPLE GO! so all the slaves follow him into the desert, then the pharaoh changes his mind and sends his *merkavot* after them, and then they're stuck at the Red Sea, and everyone starts panicking and getting mad at Moses, then Moses lifts his staff and says, 'Behold his mighty hand!' and the sea parts and all the slaves run super fast with their families and chickens and stuff, and then the pharaoh's *merkavot* chase them, and just when the last family with kids and animals gets to the end, Moses lowers his staff and the sea crashes on the *merkavot* and they drown, and the pharaoh sees it all!"

"Well, you do know the story."

"Thank you, Rabbi."

"But that's just the surface."

"It is?"

"Yes. I want you to reflect on it."

"Do I have to make a poster?"

"No. This isn't school."

"Okay, because I hate making posters."

"But I have a question for you to think about."

"Okay."

"You think about it, then write down your thoughts, then we'll discuss it."

"What if I get it wrong?"

"There are no wrong answers, Grape."

"What if I don't know?"

"Just write about what you don't know."

The rabbi was right. This wasn't like school at all.

"Here's my question. Why is the pharaoh so stubborn? After all the horrible plagues, why doesn't he just let the slaves go?"

Lou, it was a super interesting question.

"Just think about it."

"Okay."

"Now let's see how you're doing on your Hebrew. Read these two lines."

So I did.

On the ride home I opened the window, then I asked for a Mentos, but instead of eating it I dropped it in my backpack, and when we got home I ran out of the car super fast.

"¡Grape, *qué cosa!*" my mom said.

"I have to pee!" I said.

"Me, too!" my mom said.

I ran to the kitchen and put the frog head in the freezer, then I got my Evel Knievel jacket on.

"*¿A dónde vas?*" my mom said.

"The park," I said.

"No! Is a concussion!"

"But I'm not riding my bike, Mom."

"*No importa.*"

"That's not fair!"

"Betsy is coming for dinner, then *Movie of the Week.*"

"But I want to see Heidi."

"*¿Qué pasa con* the Heidi?" my mom said.

"She's my friend, Mom! I told you! She taught me how to pop a wheelie!"

"*¡Es vieja,* Grape!*"

"But she's my friend!"

Then the front door opened and I smelled my dad's ammonia blueprints.

"*¡Una hora,* Javier!*" my mom said, then he said, "*Sí, sí, qué cosa,*" and he went to his room, but instead of coming out in his robe and slippers, he was dressed kind of fancy.

"*¡Tu nariz!*" my mom said. "*¡Limpia el* sunscreen *de tu nariz!*"

She was telling my dad to clean the super-white sunscreen off his nose, then she told me to put nice clothes on.

Lou, I didn't understand. Your mom comes over all the time, and we never dress fancy unless it's for the Academy Awards, then my dad looked at me, so I went to my room and put a fancy shirt on.

Then there was a knock at the door, and I understood.

Your mom had super-red lipstick on and a fancy dress and high heels, and she had a box in her hand, and the thing is, her boyfriend was with her, and he was dressed fancy too, but it was weird because the first time I saw him he had a sweatband and his hair was long, but this time he had a beard and he was kind of bald.

"Hello, Grape," your mom said.

"Hi."

"This is Eddie."

"Nice to meet you, little man!" Eddie said.

I shook Eddie's hand.

My mom and dad said hello and shook hands with Eddie, then your mom said, "We brought a cake! We made it healthy like Jack says. No Baskin Robbins 31 Flavors nonsense here! We used coconut cream, didn't we, Eddie?"

Eddie said they did.

"I'll just throw it in the freezer," your mom said.

So that's what she did. She threw it in the freezer.

We sat down, and Eddie said, "So, Javier, how do you like the juicer?"

My dad looked at my mom.

"Is a very nice present," my mom said.

"Best three things ever happened to me," Eddie said. "Jack LaLanne, the power juicer, and this pretty lady here."

He was pointing at your mom, then he kind of poked her shoulder.

Dinner was super boring. Your mom and Eddie talked about Jack LaLanne the whole time, then your mom said, "Speaking of Jack, I believe it's time for dessert. You'll just love the coconut cream! You three sit still, and Eddie and I will do the serving!"

Lou, I was super ready for dinner to be over.

And then we heard a scream.

In the morning my mom and dad drove me to Dr. Vecchi.

They went in first, then it was my turn.

Dr. Vecchi was wearing shorts and a T-shirt, and he had stubble on his face, and there was a big thermos on his desk and a coffee cup in front of him.

I asked him if it was a tennis day.

"Yes, in fact it is."

"Oh, sorry."

"So, want to tell me what happened?"

"Um…I put a frog head in the freezer."

"I know that part, Grape. The question is, *why* did you put a frog head in the freezer?"

"Because Bully Jim cut it off."

"Still doesn't make sense," he said.

"We couldn't think of a plan."

"For what?" Dr. Vecchi said.

"To get Featherhead."

"Who's Featherhead?"

"Maxwell."

"Who's Maxwell?"

"A jerk-off jerk."

Dr. Vecchi's eyes got super wide.

"He has feathered hair," I said, "and he thinks he's cool and he brags about everything."

"And that's why you hate him so much?"

"Yes."

Dr. Vecchi drank some coffee, then he opened his thermos and poured more. "Grape," he said, "there's something you're not telling me."

"And he wears fancy disco shirts to school!"

"Grape," he said, "this frog thing. Your mom and dad are worried."

"They are?"

"It's not natural to put frog heads in freezers."

I just sat there.

"To be honest, Grape, it's the last thing your mom and dad need right now. With the baby and your bar mitzvah and your grandparents coming from so far away, everyone's a little nervous."

"Like Lou's mom?"

"Not that kind of nervous."

"Oh."

"You want to tell me what's really going on."

So I did.

And the thing is, he laughed. "Young love," he said. "Thank God."

Lou, I never heard Dr. Vecchi talk about God.

"I'm going to ask your parents in here, Grape. You have to tell them the truth."

So that's what I did. I sat in the office with my mom and dad and Dr. Vecchi and told them the truth, and my mom said, "*¡Dios mío!*" a bunch of times.

"I'm sorry," I said.

Dr. Vecchi drank more coffee, then he asked my mom and dad how they felt, and my mom said, "*¡Basta ya, Grape! Una rana! ¡Pobrecita Betsy! ¡Pobrecito Eddie! ¡Casi se mueren!*"

And then, Lou, my dad started laughing.

"Javier," my mom said, "*¡no te rías!*"

And the thing is, Dr. Vecchi started laughing too.

"*¡Qué cosa!*" my mom said, "is the Clair!" and then she started laughing, and my dad said, "Grape is a poet! He love a girl and he sings to her, and then this boy *con pelo de pájaro* take his girl, and Grape cut the frog head off!"

Everyone was laughing, Lou!

It was super cool.

Your best friend,
Grape

THe LonG SaiL

OCTOBER 27,1976

Dear Lou,

Today we met at the kitchen table for our last official meeting about The Long Sail.

My dad reminded us about checking the tailpipe thing and *over and out* and the tankers, then he unfolded the map again and showed us where we were sailing, then he asked if we had any questions and my mom said no, then I said no, then my mom told my dad to close his eyes.

"Is a surprise," she said.

My dad closed his eyes.

"*Muy bien,*" she said. "Now, open."

My dad opened his eyes.

Lou, my mom bought an official captain's hat for my dad! It was like the Skipper's hat in *Gilligan's Island*, with a white top and a black brim and a life buoy and a gold rope thing sewn on it.

"For The Long Sail," my mom said.

My dad put the hat on, and then he stood up super straight.

"How does it look?" he said.

"*Muy* handsome," my mom said.

"Grape, *mira. ¡Capitán* Javier!" my dad said.

"Cool!" I said.

He looked at my mom. "*Gracias, mi amor,*" he said, then he kissed her. "Is good to be alive! I am *Capitán* Javier, and you are First Mate Angélica, and Second Mate Grape!"

"*¡Y el* baby!*" my mom said.

"*Sí,*" my dad said, "*Capitán* Baby!"

It was super funny!

Then the phone rang, and it wasn't funny anymore.

My mom picked it up. "Javier," she said, "*es la oficina de los botes.*"

"Grape, Angélica," my dad said, "*miren la televisión.*"

So that's what we did. We watched TV.

It was *The Bionic Woman.* She was hiding behind a car listening to these two bad guys in a building super far away.

"*¿Cómo puede oír?*" my mom said.

"She has bionic ears," I said.

The thing is, I don't have bionic ears, but I could still hear my dad.

"No," he said, "is impossible! I have been a month on that boat! *Don't tell me is the best you can do!* Let me put it this way…"

The bionic woman ran to the building.

Then I heard the phone slam. "*¡Hijo de puta!*" my dad said, then he called us back to the kitchen.

"Is a new boat," he said.

"*¿Por qué?*" my mom said.

"Because the owners need it. Because is in writing that the owners can change their mind."

Lou, it's like the stupid court.

"But they find us another boat," my dad said. "Is the same."

"*Muy bien,*" my mom said.

"But is not Marina del Sol!" my dad said. "Is a monster harbor. An hour to motor out, tankers everywhere, *pero no tengas miedo.* They have their own lanes." He took his glasses off and rubbed his eyes. "Angélica," he said, "one day we buy *un bote!*"

"*Sí, Capitán* Javier."

He took his map out and made new marks for The Long Sail.

We woke up super early and found the new boat, and my dad

was right. The boat was the same, but the monster harbor was super different.

At Marina del Sol, we motor super slowly and wave at other sailors, and when a motorboat speeds by my dad gives me a thumbs-down, then my mom steers and my dad asks me to make sure water's spitting from the tailpipe thing, then he gets the sails ready, then we pass the breakers, then we get to where the pelicans fly, then my dad smiles and turns the engine off, then my mom makes me put more sunscreen on and my dad sings and sometimes gets naked.

But the monster harbor is like a city. Tankers are docked everywhere! We even saw a fancy cruise ship and passengers boarding a ramp and other passengers waving at their friends from the deck, and a million seagulls screaming and fighting for food.

"Is like a seagull tornado," my dad said.

"*Sí, Capitán*," my mom said.

"*Maneja,* Angélica."

My mom took the tiller and my dad went down the companionway to the radio, then he said, "This is *Capitán* Javier of *Playing Hooky*" because that was the name of the new boat, then he climbed to the cockpit and asked me if water was spitting out of the tailpipe thing, so I checked, and there was, so I said, "Yes, *Capitán* Javier, over!" then my dad took the tiller and said, "*Maneja,* Angélica" again, then he went down the companionway, then my mom said, "*¡Dios mío,* Javier! *Come un poco de* sandwich," but he didn't answer, then my mom said, "*Toca mi* belly, Grape, *el* baby," so I touched her belly and felt the baby kick, then my dad climbed back to the cockpit, then my mom said, "*¡*Javier, *el* baby *se está moviendo!*" but my dad didn't answer, and then, kind of far away, I saw something.

"*Capitán*," I said, "the breakers!"

I thought my dad would be excited, but he wasn't. Instead, he pointed and said, "*¡Los tigres!*"

It was super weird.

Then he did something super weirder.

He stumbled around the cockpit, then he sat on my lap.

"Javier," my mom said, "*¿qué haces?*"

"Ow," I said.

My dad stood up and pointed at the breakers.

"*¡Los tigres!*" he said again.

"*¿Cuáles tigres?*" my mom said.

"*¡Hay tigres en el cielo!*" he said.

Lou, my dad said there were tigers in the sky.

He was acting like Don Quixote.

"*¡Dios mío,* Javier!" my mom said. "*¿Qué estás decindo?*"

"*Tenemos que hablar por radio,*" he said, then he went down the companionway.

And then there was a big thump.

I ran over and looked down.

Lou, my dad was on his back, between the sink and the table, and his glasses were smashed against the side of his face, and the thing is, he wasn't moving and his eyes were closed.

"Grape!" my mom said. "*¡Maneja!*"

So that's what I did. I steered.

But the thing is, we were getting closer to the breakers and the open sea.

My mom screamed into the radio mouthpiece thing. She didn't even say her *overs*. "Mayday! Mayday! Is *Spray*. No! Is not *Spray*! *¿Dios mío, qué es?* Grape! Look on back of the boat. *¿Cuál es el nombre del bote?*"

"But, Mom, the breakers!"

"Let go and look, Grape, is okay!"

I let go of the tiller and leaned over the back of the boat.

"*Playing Hooky!*" I said, then I grabbed the tiller again.

"Is *Playing Hooky*," my mom said, "Mayday!"

"Mom! The breakers!"

She dropped the radio mouthpiece thing and took the tiller and told me to go to my dad.

So that's what I did. I went to my dad.

Then my mom said something. "Keep him awake, Grape! You have to keep him awake!"

The thing is, my dad was mumbling and his eyes were wobbling around.

"MOM!"

"Is okay, Grape! Talk to him!"

"MOM! WHAT'S WRONG?"

"Grape! *¡Que no se duerma!* Don't let him sleep! You can't let him fall asleep, Grape. He can die."

Lou, that's what she said.

"Grape! Talk to him!"

"Dad! Dad, hey, DAD!"

"*¿Qué pasa?*" my dad said.

"You fainted! Dad, you fainted!"

"*¿Dónde?*"

"In the boat."

"*¿Qué bote?*"

"*Playing Hooky!*"

"What is the hooky?"

"It was supposed to be *Spray*, but last night they called because the owner didn't want to rent it and you got super mad and they gave us this boat instead!"

The thing is, my dad wasn't listening.

His eyes were closed.

"MOM!"

"Talk to him, Grape!"

"DAD! DAD! DAD! Mom called the police!"

"*¿Qué policia?*" he said.

"She forgot to say her *overs*!"

"*¿Dónde están mis lentes?*"

"Here, Dad, your glasses are here!"

I tried to put the glasses on, but his head kind of flopped to the side, then his eyes got super sleepy.

"DAD! DAD! DAD! DAD! DAD!"

His eyes opened super wide. "Grape, *¿qué pasa?* What is happening?"

"Dad, you fainted! Mom called the police!"

"You mean the coast guard?"

"Yes! Dad! They're coming to help!"

"No! Grape! They are taking us out to sea! Don't let them take us!"

Then his eyes closed and I said DAD! a million times, but they still wouldn't open.

"MOM!"

"GRAPE!"

"DAD! MY BAR MITZVAH'S SOON!"

But my dad didn't care about my bar mitzvah. "You need to listen to me," he said. "They are imposters! They will take us out to the sea and leave us there."

I heard a siren.

"No, Dad! They're going to help."

"*¿Dónde está* Angélica?"

"She's steering, Dad!"

"Tell her not to let them on board. Use the flare gun!"

Then he closed his eyes.

"My bar mitzvah's soon! It's about Moses and the pharaoh!"

"Don't let them on the boat!"

"DAD, I'll eat radishes!"

Then I heard a loudspeaker. "Ma'am, kill your engine immediately, we're boarding on the starboard quarter."

I kept talking to my dad, then a super official coast guard guy looked down from the top of the companionway. "Get on up to the cockpit, son," he said. "Right now."

So that's what I did. I went to the cockpit right away, then I threw up a bunch of times.

When I was done throwing up, I heard counting.

"One...two...three," the coast guard guy said.

They kind of passed my dad up the companionway on a

stretcher, and the thing is, he had a breathing mask on. The coast guard tied our boat to their boat and they towed us to a dock, then they took my dad off the boat and into an ambulance, then I walked to the edge of the dock and threw up more.

"Ma'am," the coast guard guy said, "you should both be checked out, especially the boy."

At the hospital the doctor shined a little flashlight in my eyes and told me to follow her finger.

"What's your name?" she said.

"Grape."

She looked at my mom. "I think it's best if we keep him overnight—"

"It's my adopted name," I said.

"Well…okay, then. And when's your birthday?"

I told her.

"Can you tell me what happened on the boat?"

"My dad fainted."

"That must have been scary for you."

"Brutal scary," I said.

"Well, I think you're fine. Your mom told me what you did. You're a very brave boy."

"What happened to my dad?"

"Carbon monoxide built up in the boat's cabin. It poisoned your dad."

"Who poisoned him?"

"Nobody did. There was something wrong with the engine."

"Is that why he was acting so weird?"

"Yes."

"Like he has spiders?"

"Spiders?"

"And why he talked about tigers and the coast guard imposters."

"*¡Dios mío!*" my mom said. "*¡Los tigres!*"

"Yes," the doctor said, "poison does that. Hallucinations."

"Can I see him?"

"Soon."

"Will he be okay?"

"I think so."

"Go to the waiting room, Grape," my mom said. "Betsy is here."

So that's what I did. I went to the waiting room.

It was super weird. Your mom was there with her boyfriend, but the thing is, his hair was curly and gray. I thought maybe I should ask for the doctor again, then I thought about it a little.

Lou, your mom has a new boyfriend.

She also had three thermoses.

"Here you go, Grape," she said, "I juiced one for you, and I have one for your dad and your mom too."

I told her I didn't want a juice.

"How about an U-NO bar?" your mom's new boyfriend said.

"Okay," I said.

"I love U-NO bars," he said.

"Me, too."

"I got three from the vending machine down the hallway. I can get more if you want."

"Okay."

Your mom shook her head and said something about sugar, then I ate two U-NO bars, then my mom came out and hugged your mom, then my mom held my hand and we walked down the hallway.

We opened a door.

My dad was in a white robe and he had little tubes in his arms and this bag hanging on a metal thing like in *Movie of the Week*. I looked at him, and he looked at me, then he said, "*Capitán* Grape," kind of soft.

Lou, it was the first time I ever saw him cry.

My dad was in the hospital for two days. When he came home my mom kept asking him if he was okay, and he said he was, then he kept asking my mom if the baby was okay, and my mom said the baby was, then my mom kept asking if I was okay, and I said I was, then the next morning my mom said she had to take my dad to the regular doctor.

The thing is, the spiders didn't want him to go to the regular doctor.

"Grape," my mom said, "is what the hospital said. Is the carbon monoxide poisoning."

They're going to kill him, the spiders said.

"No, they're not," I said.

"Grape? *¿Con quién hablas?*"

Yes, they are.

"Shut up," I said.

You need to stop them!

"MOM!"

"*¿Qué pasa, pobrecito* Grape?"

"Don't take dad to the doctor!"

"Is okay, Grape."

"NO! You can't!"

My mom hugged me. "Is okay, Grape. *No tengas miedo.*"

¡Ten miedo! the spiders said.

"Mom?"

"*¿Sí,* Grape?"

"I need to see Dr. Vecchi."

Dr. Vecchi said I was dramatized.

"There's an emergency part of our brains," he said, "and sometimes the emergency part doesn't turn off even after the emergency's over. What you went through was very intense, so it might take a while."

The spiders didn't care.

That's not Doctor Vecchi, they said.

"Yes it is," I said.

"What's that?" Doctor Vecchi said.

"Um…nothing."

"Grape, do you really think the doctors are going to kill your dad?"

Don't answer him! He's an imposter!

"No, he isn't!" I said.

"Who isn't?"

I just looked at him.

"Grape, are you okay?"

Tell him you are!

"I am."

He talked more about the emergency part of the brain, and then he said he wants to see me twice a week.

Your best friend,

Grape

The Smoke Rings

November 8, 1976

Dear Lou,

I was finally able to see Heidi again.

"Kid!" she said, "where have you been? I missed you!"

"I had a concussion from the turtle, then we went on the long sail and my dad was poisoned and I got dramatized, and the thing is, I'm still not allowed to ride my bike."

"That's okay, kid. You can hang out with us."

So that's what I did. I hung out.

Rusty played Black Sabbath and explained the meaning of every song, then Heidi rode around and came back, then Rusty played more songs and told me to listen to the lyrics, then they smoked cigarettes and I looked for turkey vultures, then we heard the ice cream man and Heidi got us all Bomb Pops and we ate them super fast so they didn't melt, then she looked at her watch and said she had to go because her new parents were super strict, then she said, "Love you, kid," and pedaled away.

I sat there with Rusty.

He got a pack of cigarettes from his backpack, and the thing is, Lou, you would hate it because there was a camel on the cover. He peeled the plastic off, then he hit the bottom of the pack against his palm a bunch of times.

I asked him about it.

"I'm packing them," he said, "so the tobacco's even. Has to be even to get a clean smoke, man."

"Oh."

Then he did something.

He lit the cigarette and puffed on it super long, then he

clicked his jaw and blew a really big smoke ring, then he blew a smaller smoke ring through the big one!

The spiders loved it.

Did you see that?

"Yeah."

Ask him to do it again.

"Do it again," I said.

Rusty did it again, but this time he blew three rings in a row!

Ask him how he does it.

So that's what I did.

"First, I take a big hit so there's lots of smoke to work with, then I make an O with my lips, and then it's all about the clicking and the exhale, man."

"Cool."

"It's one movement, just one movement, one jaw click, but it takes a lot of practice."

"Cool."

"You have to stretch your face a lot."

"Like Jack LaLanne?"

"Huh?"

"The PE guy on TV."

"Does he blow smoke rings?"

"I don't think so," I said.

"Here, man, watch me." He took a big hit, then he did the jaw clicking thing and he blew three little smoke rings.

You need to do that, the spiders said.

Oh no.

I tried to remember what Dr. Vecchi said about the spiders. "Grape," he said, "let them talk, but don't argue, and when they tell you to do something crazy, let their words float by like clouds passing across the sky."

I tried, but the thing is, there were other clouds passing across the sky. Little cigarette clouds.

I asked Rusty to teach me.

"You might want to wait a few years, man."

"Yeah, but—"

"I'm gonna ride the gully. See you tomorrow."

"Okay."

"And think about those Sabbath lyrics. They mean something, man."

I tried to think about the lyrics, but I couldn't because, the thing is, Rusty forgot his cigarettes.

And his lighter.

Lou, it was a miracle.

Hey, Grape, do you see that?

"Yeah."

Take one.

"Okay."

Now pack it.

So that's what I did. I opened my palm and packed it, and the cigarette broke in half.

Get another one.

"Okay."

Forget about packing it.

"Okay."

Now light it.

So that's what I did. I spun the metal wheel part of the lighter and held the cigarette to the flame and sucked in, but nothing happened, then I did it again and left the flame on longer and sucked in super hard, and then something happened.

Lou, the cigarette was on fire.

I dropped it on the cement and stepped on it a bunch of times and kind of screamed.

"Hey, man! What the hell!"

It was Rusty.

"I...um...the spiders..."

"What spiders?"

"I have spiders in my brain."

"You have something in your brain, that's for sure. You lit the filter, man!"

"I did?"

"You owe me a cig!"

"Okay."

The thing is, I have no way of getting him a cig.

I started to cry.

"Hey, it's all right. I'm just kidding." He took his beanie off and sat down. "What's the matter, man?"

I told him how I was dramatized, and about Clair and Featherhead and the frogs and the court and New York and your mom being nervous.

"That's a lot, man. No wonder you want a cig."

"Thanks."

"Hey, I got a Sabbath song that will help."

Oh no.

He fast forwarded the tape, but the thing is, instead of a song with a bunch of screaming and loud guitar playing, it was super slow and sad.

"Hear that?" Rusty said. "He's going through changes. Just like you, man."

Lou, that's the name of the song, "Changes."

It's my new favorite song!

When it was over I asked him to play it again.

"Cool. Lie back this time."

"Huh?"

"Lie back, man. Just lie back and watch the sky."

So that's what we did. We lay back and watched the sky, and some turkey vultures flew over, and the singer guy kept saying, "I'm going through changes," and we listened to the song a bunch of times, then we sang the "I'm going through changes" part, and after a while the sky started to get dark.

Rusty shut off the music. "Hey, man," he said.

"Yeah?"

He had a cigarette in his mouth.

"You light this part. Not the filter."

"Oh."

"Like this," he said.

He lit the cigarette.

Then, Lou, he did something.

He passed it to me.

"Now, inhale just a tiny bit," he said.

So that's what I did.

When I got home, I went to the kitchen and asked my mom to take me to the mall.

"*¿Por qué?*" she said.

"I need to get a song."

"*¿Ahora?* Is dinner and *Movie of the Week*! Is a love story! Betsy is coming."

"Can Dad take me?"

"Dad is coming home late today."

"Is he sailing?"

"No, *pobrecito.*"

"Is he at the doctor?"

"No, *todo bien*, Grape! He's at the *oficina.*"

"Are you sure?"

"*Sí*, Grape. *Todo bien*. He has business trip soon. Is a big meeting."

"What business trip?"

"Is San Diego, Grape. Is a big contract."

"What contract?"

"*No se.* When he comes home you can ask him."

"Can you take me to the mall in the morning?"

"Is school!"

"Then after school?"

"*¡Qué cosa!*"

"It's important, Mom!"

"Is the Elton John?"

"No, Mom! Elton John sucks!"

My mom kind of looked at me. "Why is so important?" she said.

"I'm going through changes," I said.

The thing is, my mom was going through changes too. She was pregnant, and pregnant people have bionic noses.

She took her apron off. "*Ven aquí*," she said.

"Why?" I said.

"*¡Ven aquí! ¡Ahora!*"

I walked over to her, then she kind of hugged me and sniffed my face, and her belly pushed against my belly, then she put her nose on my lips, then she sniffed again, then she backed up and put her hand over her mouth like people who get dramatized in *Movie of the Week*.

"*¡Dios mío!*" she said. "Is the Heidi?"

Lou, I didn't understand.

Then there was a knock on the door.

"*¡Dios mío!*" my mom said again.

I heard your mom kind of yell, "Yoo-hoo! Yoo-hoo! It's just me and Ralph."

"Grape," my mom said, "*¡lávate la cara y las manos!*"

So that's what I did. I washed my face and hands, then I went to my room and turned the radio on and tried to find "Changes," then I gave up and tried to think about the rabbi's pharaoh question, then my mom called me to dinner.

Lou, Ralph is the man from the hospital with the curly gray hair. He was dressed super fancy, and he talked about his insurance company and gave his business card to my mom, then he asked me if I wanted one, and I told him I did, and he said, "Never too early, you know!" and kind of laughed, and every time your mom tried to talk about Jack LaLanne, Ralph said, "I would love to sell that guy a policy! He must be worth millions!"

Our moms barely talked.

It was super weird.

Then we sat on the couch and watched *Movie of the Week*.

It was super sad. The lady gets cancer and her boyfriend quits his job, then he takes her to Paris, and there's sad music, and she loses her hair. And the thing is, normally in a super sad movie my mom says, "*¿Qué cosa!*" and your mom says, "No! That can't be!" and I say, "Mom, what's going to happen?" and my mom says, "*No sé*, Grape," and your mom says, "Angélica, get the tissues!"

But this time they didn't get tissues.

They just sat there.

Ralph ate an U-NO bar and fell asleep.

Then the front door opened and I smelled my dad's blueprint ammonia, and my mom kind of shuffled off the couch and followed him to his room.

The lady was in a hospital bed now with all the tubes, and her boyfriend was crying, and he had a little statue of the Eiffel Tower, then there was a commercial, so I went to the kitchen and ate a bunch of Nilla Wafers super fast so your mom wouldn't see, then I went back to the couch, and after a while the movie ended.

"Well, Grape," your mom said, "that was a very sad movie."

"Do you want tissues?" I said.

"No, thank you."

We kind of just sat there.

Ralph snored.

"Grape, when he wakes up, tell him I made my way home."

So that's what I did. I sat on the couch waiting for Ralph to wake up.

The news came on. The main guy talked about the election. It was super boring. Ralph mumbled, then his mouth opened super wide and he kind of snorted, so I ate more Nilla Wafers, then I went back to the couch, and he was still there, so I went to my mom and dad's room and knocked.

"*¿Qué quieres,* Grape?" my mom said.

"The movie is over," I said.

"*Un momento*," my mom said.

I heard them talking in Spanish, then my mom came out. I pointed to the couch.

"*Pobrecita* Betsy," my mom said.

But I didn't care about *Pobrecita* Betsy.

"Where is Dad?" I said.

My mom kind of stared at me.

"Is fine," she said. "Dad is okay."

She woke Ralph up. He gave her another business card and left.

Then my dad came out of his room, and the thing is, he wasn't in his robe.

"Dad?"

Lou, he just left the house.

"MOM!"

"Is okay, Grape."

"Where's he going?"

"Is back soon," she said. "Now *vete a tu cuarto*. Don't worry."

So that's what I did. I went to my room and listened to the radio and tried not to worry about my dad.

After a while I heard the front door open.

I also heard footsteps.

They were coming to my room.

Usually when my dad comes to my room he knocks and I say, "Come in," then he asks how my day was and gives me a kiss and says *Let me put it this way* a few times, or if I'm in trouble or it's an official meeting, he knocks and says, "Come to the kitchen," but this time he didn't knock or say "Come to the kitchen." Instead, he opened my door and pinched my ear and pulled me off my bed all the way to the kitchen.

"Ow!" I said.

"*¡Siéntate!*" he said.

I sat down.

He closed the kitchen door, then he pulled something out of a plastic bag.

It was a little box with a camel on it.

"*Ábrela*," my dad said.

So that's what I did. I opened the box of cigarettes.

"Take one."

I took a cigarette out.

"*Métalo a la boca.*"

"Dad...I don't—"

"*¡PONLO EN TU BOCA!*"

I put it in my mouth, then he lit a match and put the flame on the cigarette.

"*¡Fuma!*" he said. "Smoke!"

"NO! DAD!"

The cigarette dropped on the table.

He picked it up and put it back in my mouth.

"*¡Quieres fumar! ¡Ahora vamos a fumar!*"

"NO, DAD, PLEASE!"

"*¡FUMA!*"

So that's what I did. I smoke-cried and coughed super hard, and when I finished coughing my dad said, "*¡MAS!*" so I smoked more, then my eyes got super watery, so I kind of spit the cigarette on the table and said, "I'M SORRY!" then my dad picked up the cigarette and put it in my mouth again and said, "*¡TERMINA!*" and then I heard my mom screaming, "*¡BASTA, JAVIER!*" and he looked at her and took the cigarette out of my mouth and turned the water on in the sink and put it out.

"You are in the ground for two weeks!" he said.

"And no more the Heidi!" my mom said.

And then I threw up on the kitchen floor.

Your best friend,
Grape

Trouble Camp

November 12, 1976

Dear Lou,

    This might as well be my trouble book again.

    "Tell me what happened," Dr. Vecchi said.

    So that's what I did. I told him what happened.

    "You know cigarettes are bad for you, right?" he said.

    "Yes."

    "And it's against the law for you to smoke?"

    "Am I going to get arrested?"

    "No, Grape, you're not going to get arrested."

    "Oh."

    "So why did you do it?"

    "I'm going through changes," I said.

    He leaned back in his chair. "Like what?" he said.

    "Um. I feel unhappy."

    "Go on."

    "I feel so sad."

    "About what?"

    "I've lost the best friend that I ever had."

    "Grape?"

    "Yes?"

    "That's a Black Sabbath song."

    Lou, Dr. Vecchi listens to Black Sabbath!

    "Oh, well, yeah. Sorry."

    "That explains the hair," he said.

    "What?"

    "Never mind. Let's get back to it. Why did you smoke?"

    "Um…I'm dramatized," I said.

    Dr. Vecchi kind of laughed. "Try again," he said.

So I did.

"The smoke rings," I said.

"Go on."

"The spiders liked them."

"That makes sense."

"Thank you."

"You know," he said, "I smoked when I was younger."

"Did you make smoke rings?"

"No. Only cool kids did that."

"Oh."

"And it was really hard to quit."

"It was?"

"Yup."

"Dr. Vecchi?"

"Yes, Grape?"

"Why did my dad get so mad?"

"A lot's going on in his life, Grape."

"Is he nervous?"

"No, not exactly. But think about it. He's got a baby coming, his parents are flying in, he got carbon monoxide poisoning, then he comes home from a long day of work to find out that you've been smoking."

We just sat there.

"Remember," Dr. Vecchi said, "your dad is also a son, and he doesn't want to disappoint his parents."

Lou, I never thought of that.

"Dr. Vecchi?"

"Yes, Grape?"

"I'm scared of him."

"He's scared of you too."

"He is?"

"You're getting older, and he's scared of the decisions you'll make, and you don't exactly have the cleanest record."

I didn't know what record he was talking about.

"Grape, just tell him you're sorry."

"I'm afraid."

"How about you write a note?"

So that's what I did. I wrote a note.

Dear Mom and Dad,

I'm sorry about the cigarette.

Your son,

Grape

At dinner, my dad was silent-mad.

I gave him the note.

He read it, but he didn't say anything, then my mom read it and said, *"Muy bien,* Grape," then in the morning my dad left on his business trip, and since I was grounded, my life was like camp again, but it was trouble camp.

The thing is, I didn't care.

I was going to be the best kid in the world.

When Bully Jim said we should cut up Maxwell's PE shorts, I said no, and when Coach Ruth said to do the six-minute run, I took my asthma pill and did the six-minute run, and when the bus dropped me off I went straight to my room and listened to my Hebrew, then when my mom said, *"Es la hora de cenar,"* I ate dinner and asked about my dad's business trip, and my mom said, *"Todo está bien con El Capitán. No tengas miedo,"* then I went back to my room and tried to answer the rabbi's pharaoh question, but I couldn't think of anything, so I wrote, "I can't think of anything," then I listened to my Hebrew again and tried to forget about Dummy Clair and Featherhead and being dramatized and smoke rings.

The thing is, I could forget about Clair and Featherhead and being dramatized and the smoke rings, but I couldn't forget about Heidi.

And Heidi couldn't forget about me.

On the third day of trouble camp, I got off the bus and heard a voice.

"Hey, kid! Kid! I miss you something brutal!"

"I miss you brutal too," I said.

"Where have you been?"

I told her.

"I'm going to kill that Rusty kid," she said.

"It was the spiders," I said.

"What spiders?"

"I have spiders in my brain."

"No, you don't, kid. No one does."

I just looked at her.

"Well," she said, "when you're not grounded, come ride again. We'll practice longer jumps."

"Um…I can't."

"You can't what?"

"I can't go to the park," I said. "I'm not allowed."

"Ever?" she said.

"I think so."

"But that's not fair."

"I know."

Heidi sat on her bike and kind of bit the side of her cheek. "That's not fair," she said again.

"I know," I said again.

"I didn't do anything wrong!" she said.

Lou, Heidi was crying.

Then she rode away.

Your best friend,
Grape

Super Confusing

November 24, 1976

Dear Lou,

Today I tried to be the best kid in the world again.
The thing is, the world has Emily Dickinson in it.
And Maxwell.
And pop quizzes on bones.
And relay races.
And Maxwell again.

In Mr. Conway's class we read an Emily Dickinson poem
about her being dead and a fly buzzing around her face, and
then it rains and all these people cry, then someone closes
the windows.
I raised my hand.
"Yes, Grape."
"How can she write a poem if she's dead?"
"That's a good question."
"Thank you."
"Thoughts, anyone?"
Clair raised her hand.
"Yes, Clair?"
"She's just pretending," she said.
"That makes sense," Mr. Conway said.
I raised my hand.
"Yes, Grape?"
"Why would she pretend to be dead?"
Featherhead raised his hand.
"Yes, Maxwell?"
"To write the poem, duh."

Some of the kids laughed.

The spiders didn't like that.

Raise your hand, they said.

I raised my hand.

"Yes, Grape?"

The thing is, the spiders didn't understand Emily Dickinson either.

Ask him to go to the bathroom.

"Um…can I go to the bathroom?"

Mr. Conway kind of just looked at me.

"The hall pass is right there, Grape, where it always is. No need to ask."

"Double-duh," Maxwell said.

Some of the kids laughed again.

In science we had a pop quiz on bones. Sherman was like the teacher's aide again, and our teacher was Mr. Bones.

In most pop quizzes the teacher says, "Pop quiz!" and the students kind of groan, then the teacher says, "Put your books away, take out a pencil and piece of paper," then the students kind of groan again.

But not Mr. Bones. Instead, he asked Sherman to pick a number between one and thirty.

"Twenty-two!" Sherman said.

"Twenty-two it is, Mr. Kaufman. Now open the roll book and find me number twenty-two."

So that's what Sherman did. He opened the roll book and found number twenty-two. "Palmer!" he said. "Emily Palmer!"

"Emily Palmer," Mr. Bones said, "stand before Mr. Bones."

Emily Palmer stood before Mr. Bones.

"The ulna!" Mr. Bones said.

Emily Palmer touched his arm.

"Oh, that tickles!" Mr. Bones said.

Sherman laughed like crazy.

"Emily Palmer," Mr. Bones said, "a number between one and thirty, please."

"Three," Emily Palmer said.

"Mr. Kaufman, find me number three!"

"Borokovich," Sherman said. "Grape Borokovich!"

I stood before Mr. Bones.

"The femur!" Mr. Bones said.

The thing is, I had no idea where the femur is.

I kind of just stood there.

"The femur!" Mr. Bones said again.

I touched his shoulder.

"Ouch!" he said.

I touched his foot.

"Ouchy-wahwah!" Mr. Bones said.

Everybody laughed.

"The *femur*, Grape," Sherman said, "not the metatarsals!"

"One more try, Mr. Borokovich!"

I touched his skull.

"Ouchy-whazoo! I need an aspirin!" Mr. Bones said.

Everybody laughed again.

"Mr. Kaufmann," Mr. Bones said, "show Mr. Borokovich the femur, please."

Lou, the femur is the leg bone.

"Now, Mr. Kaufman, kindly ask Mr. Borokovich why he isn't memorizing Mr. Bones's bones."

So that's what Sherman did.

I didn't like that.

"I *am* memorizing," I said to Sherman.

Sherman looked at Mr. Bones.

Mr. Bones shook his bones.

"But I'm not memorizing Mr. Bones," I said. "I'm memorizing Hebrew."

"Hebrew!" Sherman said.

"The thing is, my tutor Aaron was super calm and all we

did was look at car magazines and bikini ladies and talk about his girlfriend, Sasha."

Everybody laughed.

"Then Sasha broke up with him because he was too chilled out, so he quit, then I got a new tutor."

"Go on!" Mr. Bones said.

"Then Rabbi Len found out what happened."

"Oh no!" Sherman said.

"And since my grandparents are coming from Argentina and my mom's going to have a baby, we can't move my bar mitzvah."

"I see," said Mr. Bones.

"So I'm memorizing the Hebrew part instead of learning how to read it, and Rabbi Len is my tutor."

"Lucky!" Sherman said.

"Wait a moment, Mr. Borokovich. Did you say Argentina?" Mr. Bones said.

Sherman and I just looked at him.

"Borokovich suggests Russian," he said, "so this must be your mother's side, and Jewish. Most interesting…"

Mr. Bones talked about my last name for a long time.

It was super boring.

For PE we had relay races.

"Six teams, five runners per," Coach Ruth said. "Cloudy day. Let's get it done. No running in the rain. Hear my whistle, you stop."

Lou, I wished it would rain.

"First name you hear is team captain, then race in order of names. Runner one, runner two, and so on. One lap, pass baton. Any questions?"

Nobody had any questions.

I was the fifth runner on team four.

Team four was Featherhead's team.

I raised my hand.

"What is it, Grape?" Coach Ruth said.

"I, um…"

The thing is, I wanted to tell Coach Ruth that I was getting asthma, then I remembered I was going to be the best kid in the world.

"Grape?"

"Um…I have to tie my shoe."

Everybody laughed.

Maxwell said *duh.*

Coach Ruth blew his whistle.

BREEEP!

Maxwell ran super fast, then he handed the baton to runner number two and yelled at her to keep his lead, then she passed the baton to runner number three.

The relay race was super boring, so I looked up at the sky.

A turkey vulture was circling, and the thing is, it was missing a few feathers so you could see little gaps of sky in its wings, but it was flying super pretty anyway, kind of tilting and gliding and swooping, and I felt super peaceful, like when I'm underwater.

Then I didn't feel super peaceful because someone was punching me in the arm.

"Grape," Featherhead said, "the baton!"

I took the baton.

"Keep my lead, Grape! I'm way ahead. Now run!"

Lou, I ran.

And the spiders ran with me.

Hey, Grape?

"Yeah?"

That Maxwell kid is a jerk.

"I know."

He really wants to win.

"I know."

"Keep my lead!" Maxwell said.

You can't let him win, Grape.

"I can't?"

No.

"But—"

Pretend you have asthma.

"But I'm not wheezing."

Wheeze!

"Yeah, but the lead!"

Wheeze!

I tried to wheeze, but it didn't work.

Then I felt a raindrop.

Hey, Grape, did you feel that?

"Yeah."

It's raining! No running in the rain!

"Yeah, but Coach Ruth didn't whistle."

It's raining! Grape, it's raining!

And then something happened.

I finished the race.

And the thing is, Lou, we won.

And then something else happened.

Maxwell picked me up and spun me around and said he didn't know I could run so fast, like Evel Knievel, and even though that didn't make sense, and even though he was a jerk and a featherhead, and even though it started to rain, I felt kind of happy.

The spiders didn't say anything.

It was super confusing.

Your best friend,

Grape

The Thing about God

December 1, 1976

Dear Lou,

Today I met with Rabbi Len to work on my bar mitzvah speech, but we didn't work on my speech. Instead, he asked about the cigarettes.

"I'm sorry," I said.

"Why?" he said.

"Why what?"

"Why are you sorry?"

"Because I listened to the spiders when they said smoke rings are cool."

"No, Grape. I don't buy it."

"Buy what?"

"Your apology."

I just sat there.

"Let me ask you something," he said. "Before you got in trouble, did you feel sorry?"

"Um…no."

"So why are you apologizing now?"

"Because of my mom and dad," I said.

"Well, Grape, that's what I mean. It's no good."

"But Dr. Vecchi said I should apologize."

"Who's Dr. Vecchi?"

I told him.

"There's nothing wrong with apologizing."

"Yeah, but you just said—"

"But it's no good."

"Why?"

"Because you're not really sorry."

"I'm not?"

"No. You're scared, but you're not sorry."

We just sat there.

"And what's wrong with smoking?" he said. "People have been smoking for thousands of years."

"Um…it's bad for you?"

"So are a lot of things."

"Like 'preservatives, salt, sugar, and artificial flavoring'?"

He kind of looked at me, so I told him.

"I like sugar, Grape, and between us, I can't stand Jack LaLanne."

Lou, I couldn't believe it!

"Have you tried the juice?" I said.

"What juice?"

I told him.

"No, and I don't plan to."

"Because Lou's mom always makes us juice, and she even brought them to the hospital when my dad was poisoned, and the thing is, they taste horrible, and—"

"Grape, you didn't answer my question. Why is smoking bad?"

"Umm…it makes you die?"

"We're all going to die."

"But if I smoke, my mom and dad—"

"I'm not telling you to smoke, Grape."

"You're not?"

"God, no!" He took a deep breath. "So, have you thought about the pharaoh question?"

"Yes."

"And?"

"I think the pharaoh has spiders."

"That's one explanation, but it's too easy."

"Oh."

"It's like smoking."

Now I was super confused.

"You have to find your own answers, Grape. You have to make it your own."

"Rabbi?"

"Yes, Grape."

"Are you talking about smoking or the pharaoh?"

"Both," he said. "The cigarette thing, the pharaoh, all of it."

"How?"

"I don't know."

I wanted to tell him he was the rabbi.

"You have to figure it out," he said. "That's what this whole bar mitzvah business is about."

"What if I can't figure it out?"

"That's all right too."

"But my bar mitzvah's soon."

"Then you can write about how you can't figure it out."

"I can?"

"Why not?"

"Cool," I said.

We sat there more.

"Rabbi?"

"Yes, Grape?"

"How do *you* figure it out?"

The rabbi looked at me for a super long time and stroked his invisible beard, then he said something super dramatic.

"I talk to God."

"Like Moses?"

"No, not really."

"Um…"

"Not with words, Grape."

Lou, I didn't understand.

"In silence," the rabbi said.

"Rabbi?"

"Yes, Grape."

"The rabbi at sleepover camp said God has no beginning and no end."

"That's a sharp rabbi."

"Well, then, um…if God has no beginning or end—"

"I don't know the answer to that, Grape."

"You don't?"

"No."

"Rabbi?"

"Yes, Grape."

"Did Moses really part the Red Sea?"

The rabbi smiled and put his hand on my shoulder.

"What do you think?" he said.

The rabbi was super good at not answering questions.

"I don't think so," I said.

"I don't think so either," the rabbi said.

"What about the plagues?"

"I don't think those happened either."

"Then why do I have to eat radishes?"

"Radishes?"

I explained.

"That's a great question, Grape."

"The thing is, I hate radishes."

"Me too."

"Really?"

"They're disgusting."

"Brutal disgusting!" I said.

"But you know what?"

"What?"

"During Passover, I eat them. They remind me of how bitter the world is."

I just stared at him.

"It's something I decided on my own. That's what you have to find out, Grape. Find out what matters to you."

"Okay."

"And Grape?"

"Yes?"

"I have one favor to ask. I don't want you to answer me now. Just think about it."

"Okay."

"During the ceremony, I want to use your name, your real name. Will you think about it?"

I told him I would.

When I got home I went straight to my room to work on my bar mitzvah speech about the pharaoh and cigarettes, and to make it my own. I sat at my desk a super long time, but I couldn't think of anything. After a while I said, "Hey, God," then I tried to be super quiet.

Then I fell asleep.

When I woke up, I tried again. "Hey, God," I said, "it's me, Grape," and then something happened.

I heard a voice.

But it wasn't God's.

It was Heidi's.

It's not fair, she said.

I could see her riding away, and the sad look on her face, and the way she kind of bit her cheek, and all of a sudden I didn't care about the stupid pharaoh or stupid smoking.

Heidi was right.

All I did was take one stupid puff of one stupid cigarette, and my mom and dad were dramatized.

Then I heard my mom say it was time for dinner.

I went to the kitchen super slowly and sat down, then my dad said, "*¿No* Betsy *esta noche?*" and my mom said, "*No,*" and my dad said, "*Gracias a Dios,*" then my mom said, "*¿Por qué estás tan callado,* Grape?" and I just sat there and stirred my mashed potatoes, then she took her apron off and walked over to me and said, "Feel, Grape, *el bebé* is kicking!"

"Duh," I said.

"*Y* soon your *abuelo* y *abuela* come to visit."

"Double-duh," I said.

"*¿Que es el* 'duh'? *¿Y por qué no comes?*"

"I'm not hungry."

"*Tienes que comer*," she said.

"Duh."

Then I thought of something. "If I eat, can I go to the park tomorrow?"

"*¿Qué* park?" my mom said.

"*The park*, Mom!"

"No!" my mom said. "Is the Heidi and the smoking!"

"But it's not fair!"

My dad looked at me, and I kind of covered my ear.

"*No más* the Heidi!" my mom said.

I skipped my homework and went straight to bed, but the thing is, since I'd taken my God nap, I didn't sleep all night.

Your best friend,

Grape

Today was Stupid

December 5, 1976

Dear Lou,
   Today was stupid.
   We read a sad-faced lady poem again.
   I didn't understand it at all.
   Also, it rained.

   Your best friend,
   Grape

Master of My Own Ship

December 13, 1976

Dear Lou,

At lunch Sherman said I looked sad, and I said duh, then he said it's going to rain, and I said duh, then he went to play his flute and I walked around super slowly, then Bully Jim tapped me on the shoulder and said, "That Maxwell is a featherhead, we have to get him, Grapeface," and I said, "Duh, Bully Jim," then he said, "Don't call me that, Grapeface," and I said duh, then he said, "What's the matter with you?" and I said, "Who cares, duh," and the next day Mr. Conway asked me why I didn't do my vocabulary words, and I said, "I don't know," and when he said I'll have to stay in during lunch, I said, "Who cares," and instead of doing my vocabulary words, I drew a picture of Heidi floating away in a smoke ring and a bunch of dead Egyptian boys, and when Clair walked over and said, "Hey, Grape, what's wrong? You look so sad," I said, "Duh," and Clair kind of looked at me and walked back to her Maxwell table.

Then Mr. Conway came over and collected my vocabulary sheet.

The next morning I was called into Principal Whitlock's office.

"These drawings are pretty disturbing, Grape."

"You're disturbing," I said.

He put his hands behind his head and kind of rocked back and forth. "I like you, Grape," he said, "and I can see why Principal Clarkson liked you too."

"Duh," I said.

"And I can see something's wrong."

"Double-duh."

"But listen. You're a young man now, and you'll have to make a choice."

"You're not the rabbi," I said.

"What?"

"I said you're not the rabbi, duh."

"Listen, if this behavior continues, we'll have to consider—"

"Stupid Riverwash," I said.

"But I hope not," he said.

"I don't care," I said.

"I think you do," he said.

"That's because you're stupid, duh."

I thought he would call my mom and dad or scream at me, but he didn't. Instead, he unpinned the Evel Knievel poster and rolled it up and put a rubber band around it and gave it to me.

"Up to you, Grape," he said. "'Master of your own ship.'"

On the bus ride home it was raining super hard.

I put my poncho on, and when I got off the bus I walked past my house to the top of the hill and found two leaves, and the brown one was me and the orange one was you, then I set them in the gutter and followed them all the way to the storm drain across from the park.

Lou, you won.

Then I did it again, and this time I won.

I played leaf racers over and over again, and even though my poncho was leaking and my shirt was super wet and my backpack was super wet and inside my backpack was super wet, I didn't care.

When I got home my mom said, "*¡Dios mío!*" a bunch of times, then she got a towel.

"*¡Estás empapado!*" she said.

"Duh," I said.

At dinner I tried to eat but I couldn't taste anything, so I went straight to bed and waited to die.

After a while my dad knocked on the door.

"Grape, is me," he said.

I didn't answer.

He came in.

I pulled the blanket over my head and felt the edge of my bed sink, then he tapped my leg a few times.

It was getting super hot under the cover.

"Is your bar mitzvah soon," he said, "and is time to step up to the plate."

"Duh," I said.

"Is important."

"I know," I said.

"Okay."

I thought he would say *Let me put it this way* a bunch of times and explain that I'm becoming a young man, but he didn't. He just tapped my leg again and left.

Lou, I couldn't sleep, and the thing is, I was super hungry, so I went to the kitchen and got a box of Nilla Wafers and ate the rest, then I turned the radio on super soft, then I walked around my room, then I tried to sleep again, then I unrolled the Evel Knievel poster, and even though it was kind of wet, I taped it to the wall, then I lay on my bed and looked at him flying over the Earth, then I went to my desk and opened the drawer and pulled out a bunch of papers until I found it.

That's cool, the spiders said.

"Shut up," I said.

Master of your own ship!

"Shut up!"

Capitán Grape!

"SHUT UP!"

Capitán Grape, it's not fair!

"I KNOW!"

And then, Lou, I did something.

I ran out of my room and knocked super hard on my mom and dad's door.

"Grape?" my mom said. *"¿Qué pasa? ¿Estás bien?"*

"Kitchen table!" I said.

I waited in my chair.

My mom and dad were in their robes. My dad didn't even have his glasses on, and my mom's hair was super messy and she had an eye mask on her forehead.

"Grape!" she said, *"¡son las dos de la mañana!"*

"I don't care if it's the middle of the stupid night!"

"¡Qué cosa! ¡Javier, dile algo!"

The thing is, my dad didn't say anything. I thought he would slam his hand on the table, but he just sat there.

My mom took a deep breath. "Is okay, Grape. *¿Qué pasa?"*

I tried to talk, but my lips were trembling.

"I call Doctor Vecchi," my mom said.

"No," my dad said.

"NO!" I said.

We just sat there.

Then I said something.

"It's not fair."

"Life is not fair," my dad said.

"SHUT UP, DAD!"

"¡Dios mío!" my mom said.

"LOU WENT AWAY BECAUSE OF THE STUPID COURT, AND THEN I MADE A NEW FRIEND, AND EVEN THOUGH SHE'S HAD A LOT OF MOMS AND DADS AND GOES TO RIVERWASH AND SMOKES CIGARETTES, SHE'S SUPER NICE!"

"Grape!" my mom said. *"¡Qué cosa!"*

"SHE TAUGHT ME HOW TO DO AN UPHILL WHEELIE, AND SHE WALKED ME HOME WHEN

I CRASHED ON THE TURTLE, AND SHE DIDN'T EVEN GIVE ME THE STUPID CIGARETTE ANYWAY! RUSTY DID! AND YOU'RE STUPID ABOUT THAT!"

"*¡Dios mio!*" my mom said. "*¿Quien es el* Rusty*?*"

"IT WAS ONE STUPID CIGARETTE, AND I DON'T CARE WHAT YOU SAY! IF YOU DON'T LET ME GO TO THE PARK I'M NOT GOING TO HAVE A STUPID BAR MITZVAH!

"AND IF YOU MAKE ME, I'LL SAY MOSES WAS A JERK, AND, DAD, I DON'T CARE IF YOU'RE AFRAID OF ME OR IF YOU PINCH MY EAR! I WANT TO SEE HEIDI AND RIDE MY EVEL KNIEVEL BIKE AND PRACTICE WHEELIES AND JUMPS, AND IF YOU DON'T LET ME, I'M GOING TO RIVERWASH AND I DON'T CARE BECAUSE, LET ME PUT IT THIS WAY, I'M MASTER OF MY OWN SHIP!"

I slammed my hand on the table.

"*¡HIJO DE PUTA!*" I said.

Then I ran to the backyard and ripped Sigmund to pieces and sat on his broken leaves and cried and fell asleep.

When I got up, it was getting light.

I went to the kitchen. My mom and dad were still there.

"*Dios mío,*" my mom said. "*¡Estás muy sucio!*"

She kind of ran to the sink and got a towel wet and wiped my hands and face, then my dad said, "Grape, what is this *master of your own ship?*"

"It's Evel Knievel," I said. "The principal told me about it."

"Principal?" my mom said. "*¿Qué* principal*?*"

"Principal Whitlock," I said.

"Is a good principal," my dad said, then he got up, and even though I was super dirty, he hugged me. "I'm sorry," he said. "You're right, *mi hijo.*"

My mom wiped my face more.

"You will invite her," my dad said.

Lou, I didn't understand.

"The girl. You will invite her to your bar mitzvah."

"What girl?" I said.

"The Heidi," my mom said.

I couldn't believe it.

"And the Clair," my mom said.

"But not the boy *con pelo de pájaro*," my dad said.

"Now go to sleep," my mom said.

"But I have school."

"I call the school already."

I slept all morning and then I worked on my bar mitzvah speech, then I rode to the park.

Heidi was super happy to see me.

We practiced uphill wheelies and jumped four cans, and I only crashed twice, then we hung out at the upper slab, and Heidi smoked a cigarette.

I looked at her.

"Don't even think about it," she said.

"I won't."

I told her about my bar mitzvah.

"That's great, kid!"

"But you have to dress fancy."

"Okay. I can do that."

Then she got super serious. "When is it, kid?"

I told her.

"I'll be there. Don't worry."

"I won't."

"I better go," she said. "Love you, kid."

Your best friend,
Grape

My Bar Mitzvah

December 18, 1976

Dear Lou,

 I had my bar mitzvah.

 It was the best day of my life.

 It was also the new second worst day of my life.

 This morning my mom said, "Grape, the baby is kicking. Is excited for your bar mitzvah!" then she told me to eat breakfast, so that's what I did, then my grandmother combed my hair with her fingers so it didn't look shag, but her fingers were super shaky, so she got a comb, and my grandfather drank tea with a silver straw because that's what they do in Argentina, then he smiled at me and kind of winked, then I got my fancy suit on and my dad helped me with the tie, then I put my new golden yarmulke on and folded my speech in my inside suit pocket, and everyone was nervous except me.

 I was too tired to be nervous.

 The thing is, last night I was in bed and I heard a knock on my door.

 "Come in," I said.

 But nobody came in.

 It was super weird.

 Then there was another knock, and I said, "Come in" again, but nobody came in, so I got out of bed and opened the door.

 It was my grandfather. He was in his pajama pants and his undershirt that looked like a tank top, and the reason he didn't come in is because he doesn't speak English.

 "*Vamos a la cocina, mi nieto*," he said.

So that's what I did. I went to the kitchen with my grandfather.

We sat down, then he started talking. *"Escúchame, nieto, es un día muy importante, y nos da mucha alegría venir a visitarte y ver tu bar mitzvah."*

Lou, he said it was an important day, and he was super happy he could come to my bar mitzvah.

"Gracias," I said.

"¿Y por qué piensas que es un día tan importante?"

He asked me why I think it's an important day.

The thing is, it was like having an extra rabbi, but he was super serious, and he came all the way from Argentina, and it was super important to my dad, so I said, *"Porque es mi bar mitzvah,"* which didn't make any sense because he already knew it was my bar mitzvah.

He just looked at me. Then he said it was an important day because I'm becoming a young man.

"Gracias," I said.

Then he said I'm going to start helping around the house because my mom's having a baby.

"Gracias," I said, and then I kind of got up.

Then he said something else.

"Déjame decírtelo de esta manera."

Lou, *Déjame decirlo de esta manera* means *Let me put it this way* in Spanish.

Oh no.

He talked for a super long time, and every once in a while he stopped and asked me if I understood, and I said *sí*, even though I didn't, and I started to get sleepy and my head kind of fell, but he was still talking, and when he was done, he said, *"Muy bien, mi neito. Ya es muy tarde."*

I stood up.

"Pero espera un momento," he said, and he left the kitchen.

I waited.

He came back with two little boxes.

I opened one.

There was a super fancy watch in it.

"*Gracias*," I said.

Then he gave me the other little box to open.

It was a shiny golden yarmulke.

"*Póntelo mañana.*"

Lou, he asked me to wear it for my bar mitzvah.

When we got to the temple, the rabbi shook hands with my grandparents and my mom and dad, then he said he needed to talk to me alone.

"*¡Dios mío, Grape! ¿Qué pasó?*" my mom said.

"It's all right, Mrs. Borokovich," the rabbi said. "Everything is fine."

I followed him to the study room.

"Well, Grape," he said, "you did it."

"Thank you, Rabbi."

"How are you feeling?"

"Sleepy."

"You mean you're not nervous?"

I told him about my grandfather and the yarmulke.

"Well, that's a beautiful yarmulke."

"Thank you."

"How are your mom and dad doing?"

"My dad is super serious, and my mom's going to have a baby."

"You know, a lot has happened since we started."

"You mean like Lou leaving and being dramatized and smoking a cigarette and looking at car magazines instead of getting ready for my bar mitzvah?"

The rabbi laughed. "That about covers it," he said.

"But I didn't tell you about Maxwell and Bully Jim and the frog's head."

"I'm not sure I want to know," he said.

"Okay."

"But I wanted to take a moment to say how proud I am of you."

"You are?"

"Yes. You're a good kid."

"That's what Mrs. C said."

"Who's Mrs. C?"

I told him.

"Well, she's right."

"Thank you, Rabbi."

"You have your speech?"

"Yes."

"Now go get your mom and dad and meet me at the bimah."

So that's what I did.

The rabbi said a bunch of Hebrew words, then he said, "*Ha-bar mitzvah shel Gavriel* Borokovich," and I got up and took the silver pointer thing because you're not allowed to touch the paper part of the Torah, and I followed the Hebrew words, and the rabbi had to help me a few times, then he introduced my grandparents, then they walked up to the bimah, then I said a sentence in Hebrew, and they said a sentence in Hebrew, and my grandmother's hands were shaking and my grandfather was crying, and I saw my mom kind of petting her stomach, then my grandparents kissed me, then my mom and dad came up and said sentences and kissed me, then I got to sit down, and while the rabbi said some prayers I saw your mom sitting next to Ralph, and I saw Sherman with a fancy Jewish scarf around his shoulders, and I saw Bully Jim wearing a tie, and then I saw Clair next to Heidi, and they were both wearing fancy dresses.

And the thing is, it was so cool seeing Heidi and Sherman and Bully Jim and Clair that I kind of forgot it was my bar mitzvah.

"Gabriel?" the rabbi said.

I just looked at him.

"Your speech," he said.

Everyone laughed.

I got up and took the speech out of the inside suit pocket. It was about Moses and Pharaoh and Evel Knievel and smoking and being dramatized.

Then I did the thank-you part.

It was like I won Best Picture in the Academy Awards.

When it was over I carried the Torah down the aisle and everyone clapped and sang, then we went to the back room and said a prayer for the bread, then we passed around a big loaf and took turns ripping off a piece and eating it, then we said a prayer for the wine and the grown-ups drank wine, and the kids drank grape juice, then we said another prayer and everyone hugged my mom and dad and said *mazel tov*, then Sherman said, "Fine bar mitzvah, Grape. Your speech was rather unconventional, but then again, so are you! How you brought Evel Knievel into the Moses story and the different kinds of stubbornness...well...like I said, unconventional, but interesting! Anyway, *mazel tov!*"

Bully Jim said, "Cool bar mitzvah, Grapeface."

Clair said, "Congratulations, Grape."

Then Dr. Vecchi walked over. "Great job!" he said.

"Thank you."

"I'm proud of you, Grape."

"I'm proud of you too," I said.

Then I saw Heidi. Her dress had red and white flowers on it, and her hair was down, and it was super cool because she was touching my mom's belly and laughing.

"Hi, Heidi."

"Hi, kid! That was great!"

"Thanks. Did you like the Evel Knievel part?"

"It was awesome!"

"*Sí*," my mom said, "is awesome!"

Lou, it was brutal awesome.

The party was at a fancy hotel. I got my own table with
Sherman and Bully Jim and Clair and Heidi, and my presents
got their own table, and people kept coming over and
congratulating me, and the band leader introduced me and
everyone clapped, then he introduced my mom and dad and
everyone clapped, then my dad took the microphone and
said how happy he was, and how it's a good day to be alive,
then he talked in Spanish, and I was worried he would say *Let
me put it this way*, but he didn't, then the band leader said, "It's
chair time!" then they played music and I sat in a chair and
everyone lifted me up and down, and it was super fun, then
he said lunch was being served.

Lou, lunch was super fancy, but Sherman was super weird.

The thing is, he kept leaving the table, then coming back,
then smiling, then leaving, then coming back, then smiling
even longer, then he kind of fell off his chair, then he
got up and put a napkin on his forearm and pretended to
have an English accent, then he said, "My dear Clair, may I
recommend the *escargot*?" and Clair kind of looked at him,
then he said, "And you, Master James, what can I get you
from our fine menu?" and Bully Jim shook his head, then
Sherman said, "And you, my dear bike-riding lady, might I
interest you in our latest cabernet?" to Heidi, then he left.

"Your friend is brutal weird," Heidi said.

"He is weird," Bully Jim said, "but he's also drunk."

After lunch it was time for dancing!

The band played a Hebrew song and everyone held hands
in a circle, then my dad got in the middle and danced and it was
super funny, then they played AM music and Heidi danced
with my mom and kept rubbing her belly, then I danced
with Clair, then Drunk Sherman danced with Dr. Vecchi's
wife, then I danced with my mom, then the band leader said,
"Wow, we have some *fancy* moves going on!" and everyone

stopped because, the thing is, your mom was dancing with Ralph, and Ralph's shirt was kind of unbuttoned and he had a gold chain and they were dancing ooh-la-la, then he twirled her around and pointed at the ceiling.

"*¡Dios mío!*" my mom said, "is the disco dancing!"

Everyone clapped and watched them dance, then something happened.

Drunk Sherman got between them and started unbuttoning his shirt! I was worried that his scar thing would show, and I thought Ralph would push him away, but he didn't, and everyone was laughing super hard and clapping!

Hey, Grape! the spiders said.

"I know!" I said.

I unbuttoned my shirt and danced with Drunk Sherman and your mom and Ralph, and then, guess what?

My dad unbuttoned his shirt and did some super fancy disco moves!

And then, Lou, everyone was doing disco moves, and when it was over everyone clapped, and then the band leader said, "Well, that's the highlight of my career, but let's tone it down a little, shall we?"

My mom slow-danced with my dad, and my grandparents slow-danced, and Dr. Vecchi slow-danced with his wife, and I sat there and looked at Clair, but she wasn't looking at me, and I got nervous, then I felt a tap on my shoulder.

"Dance with me, kid?"

So that's what I did.

I danced with Heidi.

It was super cool.

The rest of the party was super fun, even though the band wouldn't play "Changes." Bully Jim had to drag Drunk Sherman out from under the table, then I went outside with Heidi while she smoked a cigarette and waited for her ride.

"That was brutal fun, kid."

"Thank you."

"Your mom's so nice."

She took a puff of her cigarette, and everything got super quiet.

I looked over.

Lou, Heidi was crying.

"I went to court," she said.

"You did?"

"I have a week, kid."

"That's not fair!" I said.

"I'm going to live with my sister."

"You can live with us!" I said. "I'll tell my dad to make a bunk bed, and—"

Heidi kind of laughed.

"No, kid," she said.

"Why not?"

"Just no."

I sat there.

"I'll write you," she said.

"Okay," I said. "I'll write you back."

"That's my ride. See you tomorrow."

A car pulled up.

"Love you, kid."

"Love you, too, Heidi."

Your best friend,
Grape

Sophia of the Wind

December 23, 1976

Dear Lou,

This morning there was a knock on the door.

It was your mom, but she didn't have her Jack LaLanne outfit on, and the thing is, she was super happy. She gave my mom a hug and a bunch of kisses on the cheek, then she gave me a hug and a bunch of kisses on the cheek, then she walked back to my mom and kissed her belly, then she said the coolest thing ever.

"Lou's coming home! For two weeks!"

"*¡Muy bien!*" my mom said.

"Cool!" I said.

Then she knelt down and kissed my mom's belly again and said, "Do you hear that, little baby? Lou's coming home!"

It was super funny.

"And you know what, little baby?" your mom said.

"No," my mom said, "*¡díselo al* baby, Betsy!*"

"I'm going to spoil him rotten!"

"*¡Muy bien!*"

"No more of those stupid juices!" your mom said.

"*¡Gracias a Dios!*" my mom said.

Then your mom handed me a piece of paper.

"Here's Lou's number," she said. "Grape, you should call him."

So that's what I did. I went to the kitchen and closed the door and dialed. It rang a few times, then your dad's voice said he wasn't home and to leave a message after the beep.

So that's what I did. I left a message.

"Hi," I said, "this is Grape," then I hung up, and since

I didn't have to practice my Hebrew or think about the pharaoh or cigarettes, I went to my room and played with the timer on my new watch, then I heard our moms laughing, so I went to see what they were laughing about.

They were watching *Gilligan's Island.* My mom kept saying, "*¡Qué cosa, este Gilligan!*" Then there was a commercial and your mom told me to try to call you again.

I went to the kitchen and closed the door and dialed, but it was still your dad saying to leave a message. "Hi," I said, "this is Grape again," then I hung up and I rode my bike around.

When I came back, your mom said I should try again.

This time your dad answered.

"Hello?"

"Can I talk to Lou?"

"Lou's not home. Who is this?"

"Um…it's Grape."

"You mean that Gaby kid?"

I didn't say anything.

"Lou's at the club."

"Oh. Um…when will he be home?"

"Soon," your dad said. "Fifteen minutes or so."

"Okay. Bye."

I set my watch timer to fifteen minutes and waited.

Then something weird happened. I heard my mom kind of laughing-crying and your mom telling her to practice her breathing, like they were watching Jack LaLanne instead of Gilligan.

Then my watch beeped.

I dialed.

Your dad picked up.

He was super mad. "You just called!" he said.

"Um…you said Lou would be home in fifteen minutes, and the thing is, I have this fancy new watch with a timer, so I set it for fifteen minutes, and when it beeped I dialed again."

"Well, he's not here!"

"Um…do you know—"

"Listen, how about he calls you when he gets back?"

"Okay," I said.

I hung up and I heard more laughing-crying, but it was louder this time, then the spiders thought of something.

Hey, Grape?

"Yeah?"

What if he doesn't have your number?

"Who doesn't?"

Lou.

Oh no.

"*¡Dios mío!*" my mom said.

"Breathe!" your mom said.

Call him again! the spiders said.

Your dad answered.

"Um…I'm sorry," I said, "the thing is, I wasn't sure if Lou had my phone number."

"You've got to be kidding me," your dad said.

I told him I wasn't.

"You're his best friend," your dad said, "of course he has your number."

Lou, that was the nicest thing your dad ever said.

"But how about you give it to me just in case?"

"Okay," I said.

But I wasn't able to give it to him. The thing is, my mom wasn't laughing-crying anymore. She was screaming. "GRAPE!" she said, "*¡Habla* a *tu papa! ¡Ya viene el* baby! *¡SE ROMPIÓ LA FUENTE!*"

"What the hell is going on?" your dad said.

"Oh, um…sorry…the thing is, my mom is super pregnant and Lou's mom is telling her to breathe, and the thing is, I have to call my dad—"

"GRRRAAAYYYPE!" my mom said.

I hung up and called my dad.

A lady answered.

"Um…I need to talk to my dad, over."

"Who's your dad?"

"*Capitán* Javier, over."

"Who?"

"Um…Javier."

"Oh, sure. I'll transfer you to his line."

"Hello, is Javier," my dad said.

"DAD, IT'S GRAPE! MOM'S HAVING THE BABY! I THOUGHT IT WAS JACK LALANNE BECAUSE BETSY IS HERE BUT IT WASN'T! SHE SAID SOMETHING ABOUT WATER!"

Then your mom grabbed the phone from me.

"Meet us at the hospital," she said.

Your mom drove my mom's car, and my mom kept grunting, and your mom drove super fast and honked and said, "Learn how to drive!" then we got to the hospital and your mom asked my mom if she could walk, and my mom said no, then your mom told me to run inside and find her a wheelchair.

So that's what I did. I ran up and down the hallway until a nurse asked if she could help me.

"My mom's having a baby! She's in the parking lot with Lou's mom and we need a wheelchair!"

"Your mom's *where*?"

"In the parking lot with Lou's mom!"

She called over a worker guy and told him to get a wheelchair.

Then I heard my dad's voice.

"Grape, *¿dónde está* Angélica?"

A minute later my dad was pushing my mom in the wheelchair and my mom was grunting and saying *¡Dios mío!*, then she said, "*espera un segundo*, Javier."

My dad stopped pushing her.

She told me to come over.

"Is okay, Grape," she said, and she hugged me.

Then my dad pushed her down the hallway.

I sat in the waiting room with your mom.

"This is where Lou was born," she said.

"Cool."

My dad came back and sat with us.

"*Gracias*, Betsy," he said. "Is early, the baby."

"I think the baby wants to meet Lou," your mom said.

We waited a super long time. My dad walked back and forth and took his glasses off and rubbed his eyes, then he got coffee from the machine and your mom got a Mountain Dew, and the news was on TV. Then your mom left and came back with a worker guy who changed the channel to *The Bionic Woman*, and my dad kept walking around, then he said he had to make a phone call, then your mom said she's going to the cafeteria. She came back with sandwiches and said my dad needs to eat, so my dad ate, then he got more coffee, then a nurse came in and told my dad to follow her.

A few minutes later, he came back and told me to follow him.

My mom was in the hospital bed, but she didn't have any tubes. Instead, she had a baby.

"*Mira*," she said, "*es* Sophia."

Lou, I have a little sister!

She was wrapped in a blanket and her eyes were closed and she only had a little hair.

"*Siéntate allí*, Grape," my dad said.

I sat down.

Then my dad did something.

He scooped up Sophia and brought her over to me and put her in my arms.

"A little early," my dad said.

"Betsy said she wants to meet Lou," I said.

My mom laughed.

"*Tranquila*, Angélica," my dad said.

"*Sí, mi amor.*"

"A little early," my dad said again, "but she is even and strong."

"Like the wind," I said.

"*Sí*, Grape. *Como el viento.*"

Sophia of the Wind.

Lou, when you come home we can take her to the park and push her around in her stroller, and I can show you how I pop a wheelie.

Your best friend,
Grape

acknowledgments

Jaynie Royal, thank you for believing in Grape and letting him tell more stories. Thank you also for your tireless work in making Regal such a rich community. David Howard, *muchisimas gracias, mi amigo*, for your help with Grape's Spanish. May the spirit of *La Bufadora* bless and keep you. Ziv Tarsi, *todo rabah*, cousin, for your help with the Hebrew. I will forever know, along with *rubber band*, how to say *chariot* in Hebrew. Gayle Brandeis, Johnston sister, thank you thank you thank you for your clear eye and generous spirit. Allison Olsen, your support of all things *Grape!* has meant so much. Who's to say...he may one day tell of a lost ticket at a Bruce Springsteen concert. And Jaymie, well, you know.